Daddy Wanted

Renee Andrews

Recycling programs
for this product may
not exist in your area.

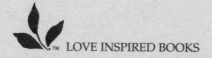

™ LOVE INSPIRED BOOKS

ISBN-13: 978-0-373-81817-4

Daddy Wanted

Printed in U.S.A.

"Why didn't you kiss me?"

The old Brodie wanted to answer, "I have no idea, but I'll make up for that now." Then he'd kiss her.

He reined in that impulse. He'd changed. But the fact that Savvy looked at him as though she might be bothered he hadn't kissed her wasn't making this any easier.

"I," he started, taking a seat on the step beneath hers and focusing on the words he should say, "I didn't want to mess up what we have going now, taking care of the kids together, by doing something that wouldn't be smart. I'm trying to do the right thing."

"You're trying to do the right thing," she repeated.

Brodie nodded, but didn't miss the fact that she sounded disappointed. Brodie was disappointed, too. But that didn't change his mind. Kissing Savvy would be a mistake, and he'd made that kind of mistake before. He wouldn't do it again, especially not with someone he cared about as much as he cared about Savvy. And he did care about her. And Dylan. And Rose and Daisy.

He had to remember all of them to control the impulse to do something he might regret. Something that would cost him another friendship.

Renee Andrews spends a lot of time in the gym. No, she isn't working out. Her husband, a former All-American gymnast, co-owns ACE Cheer Company. Renee is a kidney donor and actively supports organ donation. When she isn't writing, she enjoys traveling with her husband and bragging about their sons, daughter-in-law and grandsons. For more info on her books or on living donors, visit her website at reneeandrews.com.

Books by Renee Andrews

Love Inspired

Visit the Author Profile page at Harlequin.com for more titles.

I will not leave you as orphans; I will come to you.
—*John* 14:18

For Alanus and Jerry, our grandboys, and for all other children whose birth parents go to Heaven too early. I pray each child who loses his or her parents finds a new mommy and daddy who love them as much as your new mommy and daddy love you. Pops and KK thank God for putting you in our life, and we love you…big as the sky, to the moon and back!

Chapter One

The wild child of Claremont, Alabama, had come home.

Raised brows and muted whispers accompanied Savvy Bowers as she crossed the town square that shaped the memories of her youth, as if the giant oaks and three-tiered fountain centering the place whispered the obvious…

She's back.

Savvy opened the door to Bowers Sporting Goods as an attractive white-haired lady started out. Like that of the others Savvy had passed on her walk to her grandparents' store, the woman's expression changed as she undoubtedly put a name with the face.

"Why, Savannah Bowers, it's been a long time, dear. And you're as pretty as you were in high school." She smiled, her green eyes holding nothing but compassion toward Savvy, a welcome change from the reception she'd received so far.

It only took a moment to recognize Ms. Martin. Her hair had transitioned from blond to snowy white, but other than that, the lady looked practically the same as she had fifteen years ago, when Savvy had graduated from high school, kicked the north Alabama dust from her heels and headed to Panama City Beach.

Ms. Martin's son had been in Savvy's class at school until the sixth grade, when Savvy had been held back a year and he and the rest of her friends had moved on to junior high. "It has been a while," she agreed.

"I heard about you coming back to town and how you're looking after Wendy Jackson's children. I was so sad to hear about her passing. They said she fell hiking at Jasper Falls?"

"She did." Savvy's throat thickened. She hardly recognized the name Wendy Jackson. Her friend had been Willow for as long as she could remember. Willow had despised her birth name almost as much as she'd despised the parents who gave it to her, probably the reason she'd left her children to Savvy.

"Such a shame," Ms. Martin said. "Thirty-two years old. So young."

A year younger than Savvy.

"Savvy? Hey!" her grandmother's cheery voice called from the back of the store.

Thankful for a reason to end this awkward conversation, Savvy turned. "Good to see you, Ms. Martin," she said, and then stepped inside the store.

Savvy liked Ms. Martin, but she wasn't ready to tackle a discussion about Willow's death or the fact that she was expected to raise her children. Dylan, at thirteen, was angry his mom was gone. Rose and Daisy, Willow's six-year-old twins, were confused and heartbroken. And Savvy didn't know how to handle any of it.

In the past week, she'd learned of Willow's death, found out she was responsible for three children and abruptly traded life at the beach for life in the town she'd firmly left behind. And this morning's meeting with Dylan's school principal, who informed Savvy that she believed it would be "in his best interest" if they "retained" him a year, had done nothing to lift Savvy's spirits. No child should be punished because his mother died. Savvy knew that better than anyone.

Jolaine Bowers closed the distance between them, embraced her and brushed a quick kiss against her cheek. "We thought you were coming in earlier. I'm afraid your granddaddy left to go check on things at the fishing hole."

Savvy inhaled the familiar sweet scent of her

grandmother's favorite shampoo and remembered all of those hugs she'd distributed throughout her childhood. And her teens. When she told them she was moving back to Claremont, her grandparents had graciously told her she could work here again, the same way she had done in high school. She should've been here early this morning, but after Willow's kids had gotten on the bus and Savvy was alone for the first time since she'd arrived, she'd spent a good hour crying.

Then she'd reviewed the papers she'd gotten from the attorney, organized all the casseroles the church brought after the funeral and received that call asking if she could come to the school. "I should've phoned you," she said.

"Hey, it's fine. I know you've got a lot on your plate. Your granddaddy can see you tomorrow." She eased away from Savvy enough to display her trademark wink. "We're just so glad to have you back home and working at the store."

"Thanks," Savvy said, because saying she was glad to be back would be an outright lie.

Not wanting to get into any of that right now, Savvy started toward the checkout area to look for her grandfather's habitual to-do list. Finding it, she glanced at the top. "I'll get started on the new baseball inventory and—" The front page of a newspaper on the counter caused her words to lodge in her throat. She'd seen the same paper earlier today at Willow's place. Not today's paper—the date on it was March 5, from over a month ago.

Willow had saved it, too.

Her grandmother hurried to see what held Savvy's attention. "It isn't fair, is it?"

"Isn't fair…?" Savvy asked, momentarily mesmerized by the photo of the handsome man centering the page.

"That men get better looking as they age." Jolaine tapped the picture. "I meant to mail that paper to you. I remembered how close you, Willow and Brodie were in high school and thought you'd like to see what he's up to now."

Savvy stared at the broad grin and deep dimples she remembered, but instead of his Claremont High baseball cap, he wore a Stockville College one. And her grandmother was right; Brodie looked even better now. Dark eyebrows drew attention to intense eyes framed with equally dark lashes. A straight nose, strong jaw, cleft chin. The photo was in black-and-white, but Savvy knew if it were in color, icy blue eyes would peer out from that thick fan of black lashes.

In high school, Savvy and Willow had put the guys they knew in one of two categories: boys and men. The classification had nothing to do with maturity and everything to do with appearance. Some guys had a boyish look as a teen, and the majority of them outgrew that as they got older. Others looked like men from the get-go. *That* was the type that attracted Savvy and Willow.

And *that* was Brodie. Strong. Masculine. Muscled well beyond his age. From the broadness of his shoulders in the photo and the fact that he had an athletic position as head coach of the Stockville College baseball team, she'd guess those muscles were still enough to make a girl's breathing hitch.

He'd had that effect on both Willow and Savvy, even if they'd agreed they'd never act on the attraction. A common understanding between all three of them—the "wild ones"—was that they would never risk their unique relationship by crossing the boundaries of friendship. They were too much alike, their histories too similar, and they needed each other as confidants. They'd never jeopardize that. Or so the trio had promised.

But then that had changed. Willow had never forgiven him for what he'd done, nor had Savvy. Yet for some reason, Willow had saved that article.

Under the photo, the caption read Hometown Hero Brodie Evans is Back.

Savvy had already perused the story, which briefly told of Brodie beginning as a star pitcher for Claremont High, his years at the University of Tennessee, his brief stint in the majors and his new role as head coach at Stockville Community College. Twenty miles away.

Not far enough.

"You can have that copy," her grandmother said, jarring her back to the present.

Sighing, Savvy took another glance at the article, folded the paper and held it toward Jolaine. "I saw it at Willow's, but thanks for thinking of me. Do you want to keep it?"

Her grandmother's mouth opened, and then she shrugged. "No, I don't guess so."

"Okay." Savvy plunked it in the nearest trash can, then started on the baseball inventory.

Brodie Evans trudged through the locker room at Stockville Community College and reluctantly entered his office. He prayed no one had tossed the envelope while he'd been away and, inspecting the top of his desk, feared the worst.

Willow's letter was nowhere to be seen.

"Coach Evans, it's good to have you back," Phillip Stone, Brodie's assistant coach, stepped into the office. He was twenty-three, fresh off his college baseball career, and he reminded Brodie of the guy he'd been ten years ago. Young. Athletic. Charming. Someone who had the world at his fingertips. But unlike Brodie, Phillip didn't appear the kind of guy who would leave his loved ones behind while he fought to achieve his goals. "You planning to be at tonight's work-outs?" he asked.

Brodie had taken the head coaching job in January, only three months ago, and he hadn't planned to miss an entire week of workouts and practices, but his priorities had taken a tailspin when he learned his daughter had been in a wreck that had nearly taken her life. Thankfully, the doctors—and God—had pulled Marissa through, but nearly losing her had caused Brodie to real-ize the truth.

He had earned no place in her world.

"Coach?" Phillip repeated, then shook his head ruefully. "Aw, man, I'm sorry. I should've asked first. Everything okay with the family emer-gency?"

Family emergency. That was the only rationale Brodie could come up with to explain why he'd had to leave for spring break instead of stick-ing around for the team's extra practices. He'd never mentioned his daughter to the guy. Then again, that precious fifteen-year-old with his eyes technically wasn't "his daughter" anymore. Once they'd known Marissa would make it, his ex-wife, Cherie, had been quick to remind him that he'd terminated parental rights thirteen years ago.

"Coach...?" Phillip prodded.

"The emergency is over," Brodie lied. Truth-fully, his life was one big crisis now. The only daddy Marissa knew was the one who'd raised her, the one who'd married Cherie over a decade ago. But that didn't negate the fact that she was Brodie's flesh and blood.

He had to show Cherie that he was worthy of a place in his daughter's world. And he'd made a promise to himself—and more important, to God—that he would rectify past mistakes.

"There was a letter," he said gruffly, "on my desk. I'm certain it was here." He lifted the stacks of upcoming schedules and camp information, pushed aside the playbooks and still…nothing.

"A recruitment letter? I took that template and handed it over to Coach Yates while you were gone so he could follow up with those players you'd contacted."

"No, not the recruitment letter." Brodie scrubbed a hand down his face, felt the evidence of forgetting to shave this morning. "This one was…" He paused, not sure how much he wanted to divulge, and finally settled on "personal."

"Vern and his maintenance staff have been in several times cleaning up. I believe your new mail is in your slot." Phillip pointed to the incoming mail bin near the door.

Brodie hadn't thought to check the bin, stuffed full with a collection of equipment magazines, manila folders and assorted envelopes. He moved toward the container, grabbed the mass from inside and dropped the contents on his desk.

"Need help finding what you're looking for?" Phillip asked.

"No." Brodie tossed envelope after envelope until, at the bottom of the stack, he saw Willow's letter. He clutched it like a lifeline, or more accurately, like a mistake he desperately needed to fix. He'd wronged a friend and ended up losing two in the process. He'd never heard from Savvy after that night either, and he had no doubt why.

She knew what he'd done.

He stuffed the letter in his jacket pocket. "I won't make workouts tonight." Brodie glanced up to see Phillip frowning, undeniably confused at the lack of commitment shown by the college's new head coach. Brodie *was* committed to the Stockville baseball program, but if he wanted a relationship with Marissa, he had to grow up. Change. Become the father she deserved.

During the entire drive home from that Knoxville hospital, he'd begged God to show him how to do that. And God had put Willow's letter on his heart.

"I've got something I need to do, but then I'll be back with the team 24/7." He didn't know why he offered an explanation. He was the head coach, after all, and as such, he didn't have to justify himself to any of the assistant coaches. But Phillip

Stone was a great coach and a good guy, too, and Brodie wasn't going to do good people wrong, not anymore.

Understanding dawned on the young man's face. "Unfinished business with the family emergency. I gotcha. Don't worry about the team, Coach. We'll have them ready for you tomorrow." Then he left Brodie's office and disappeared through the locker room.

Exhaling slowly, Brodie withdrew the letter from his jacket, opened it and read Willow's words again. She needed to talk to him. Her son was having a tough time in school, and she wanted Brodie to tutor him.

He hadn't even realized she still lived in Claremont, or that she knew he coached at Stockville. But she mentioned an article from the Claremont paper. There wasn't a lot of stuff that happened in or around Claremont, Alabama. A local boy who'd semi made it coming back to take the head coaching job at the nearest college was apparently front-page news. And evidently, the article also discussed the fact that he was part of a mentorship program with local community kids that involved tutoring and recreational activities.

So Willow asked if Brodie could tutor her boy, but Brodie didn't know how he would face her after the way he'd left her in Knoxville.

Closing his eyes, he prayed, *God, please,*

forgive me for ignoring this for the past three weeks. Help me find the strength to see Willow again, and to apologize for being such a— The word that came to mind didn't belong in a prayer. *Such a jerk back then. And, Lord, if it be Your will, let me fix my past mistakes. Let me have some small place in my daughter's life.*

He opened his eyes, folded the letter and slid it back in the envelope. Willow needed his help. Three weeks ago, he'd avoided her, but now he wanted to make amends. And he'd start with words he'd never uttered before. But he'd say them today.

I'm sorry. And then… *Forgive me.*

To keep her mind off Willow, the children and Brodie Evans, Savvy delved into the boxes and itemized lists defining the new shipments her grandparents had received over the past week. She didn't stop for lunch or for breaks. And when her phone buzzed loudly in her jeans, she was so preoccupied, she almost fell off the tiny stool she used while sorting through the bins.

She slid it out of her pocket and answered, "Hello?"

"Savvy, hey, it's Mandy." Mandy Brantley had kept Willow's children until Savvy arrived in town yesterday afternoon, and she'd helped

Savvy get them ready for bed last night before heading to her own home.

Savvy's pulse started racing, probably because the last time the other woman had called, she'd informed Savvy that her friend was dead and that Savvy was now responsible for her three children. "Mandy, is everything okay?"

"I believe so," she replied. "But I'm just wondering… Where are you?"

"I'm at the sporting-goods store," she said. "Remember, my job started today?" She was certain she'd told her about it last night.

"I remember," Mandy said, "but you're only working until the kids get out of school, right? When I asked if you needed me to help you with them in the afternoons, you said you'd be home by the time they get off the bus each day."

Savvy took the phone from her ear and glanced at the time on the display. "Uh, what time do they get home, again?" She'd arrived in town late yesterday after they'd already gotten home from school, and Mandy had been there.

"The bus drops them off at two forty-five."

The time on Savvy's phone showed two-forty. "Oh, no! I'm not going to make it. I've got to get down there, Mandy!" She grabbed a baseball cap from a box nearby and put it on her head. It wasn't a foolproof way to disguise her from the nosy folks in Claremont, but she wasn't in the mood for more stares and whispers as she went about her business. Hurrying, she shuffled through the store aisles toward the entrance and knocked a fishing rod off the wall in the process. She picked it up and quickly returned it to the display hook.

"How could I have forgotten about the kids already?" she asked.

"Don't be so hard on yourself, Savvy. These things happen," Mandy answered.

Savvy made it to the front of the store, pushed the door open and called to her grandmother, "I've got to go. It's time for the bus!"

She glanced down to press the end button on the phone, but halted when she ran face-first into a brick wall. Or rather, a hard-plated chest that *felt* like a brick wall. "Excuse me." She looked up, and her heart lodged in her throat.

The newspaper photo didn't do him justice.

Brodie Evans was taller—a couple of inches taller—than she remembered. His eyes an even more distinctive icy blue. And the five-o'clock shadow only intensified the strength of his jaw.

"Savvy?" he questioned, and she realized he'd grabbed her forearm when she slammed into him and he'd yet to let go, the warmth of his hand seeping into her skin. "You're back," he said. "I had no idea."

"I've gotta go." She pulled her arm away, a mix of panic and anger and disappointment flooding her as she remembered how close they'd been once upon a time, and how he'd thrown it all away.

"But I was coming to your grandparents' store to find…" he began.

"They can help you with whatever you want." She forced her feet to move away from the distraction of Brodie Evans and then prayed he got everything he needed from the store today. She didn't want to talk to him again, didn't want to see him again. Turning, she sprinted across the square toward her truck, but then heard Mandy yell, "Savvy, wait!"

In the shock of seeing Brodie, she'd forgotten to disconnect the call. "What is it?" she asked breathlessly.

"I'm here, at the trailer. I was bringing a couple more casseroles from the ladies at church, so I'll wait for the kids to get off the bus, and then I'll stay until you get here."

"You're there?" she asked. But even if she didn't have to race to the bus stop, she still wanted to leave the square. And the man from her past. "Okay, but I'll be there soon." Savvy blinked past the emotions spreading over her like wildfire.

Brodie. After all these years…

A large palm cupped her left shoulder as she reached her truck. She'd been running, her chest pulling in air from the effort, and he wasn't even breaking a sweat. "Savvy, wait. I'm trying to find

Willow." Brodie turned her to face him. "I *have* to find her."

Savvy's hand squeezed the phone still pressed against her ear. Mandy said something, but she couldn't make out the words, the jolt from Brodie's statement drowning out every sound except the thudding of her heart pulsing in her ears. "Willow?" she whispered as visions of her beautiful friend flooded her mind.

Willow standing beneath Jasper Falls, her long dark hair framing a laughing face as she splashed Brodie and Savvy. Willow had *died* there, at the place they'd all loved. And Brodie had no idea.

"Yes, Willow," he said. "She wrote to me, said she needed to talk to me about helping…"

Savvy shook her head, didn't listen to anything else. "You can't help." The memory pushed tears forward, and they spilled onto her cheeks. Savvy brushed them away. "Willow's gone."

"What do you mean, she's gone?" He reached into his jacket and withdrew an envelope. "She wrote to me and said she still lived in Claremont and that she wanted to talk to me. She gave me her phone number, but her voice mail box is full. And she didn't give an address. I thought maybe your grandparents could help me find her."

"Brodie, you don't—"

He held up a hand. "Listen, Savvy, I'm sure she told you what happened, and I know you're probably still angry over what I did. But I know Willow is here, and I'm going to see her."

"No...you're not." Disbelief and shock swirled together to make her light-headed. She grabbed the truck door and took a deep breath.

"Savvy, you can't keep me from seeing her."

"I am still angry," she finally said, wanting to hit him for the way he had hurt Willow back then. She lifted her arm to do just that, but then dropped it to her side. What good would it do?

"I need to talk to her. I need to apologize," he said thickly, as though either of those things could actually happen.

Savvy gawked at him. "You're too late. It's too late to apologize. Willow—" She couldn't hold back the truth. "Willow's dead, Brodie." His eyes widened, the blow of the news evident, but Savvy had neither the time nor the inclination to explain. "And I've got to go take care of her kids." She twisted away, hurriedly climbed into her truck and slammed the door. Then she drove away without looking in the rearview mirror.

Mandy's voice echoed through the line of the phone Savvy had tossed on the seat. "Savvy?" she asked. "Savvy, can you hear me?"

She had obviously touched the speaker button at some point. Reaching for the phone, she nearly sped through the stop sign at Maple and Main before slamming on the brakes. They squealed in protest, and the phone slid toward the passenger door.

Mandy yelled, "What happened?"

Savvy held her foot firmly on the brake while she retrieved the phone. Then she answered, "It's okay, Mandy. I'm on my way."

"I figured that part out," she said. "That was Brodie, wasn't it? Is *he* okay? And are you?"

"No," she said honestly. "And no."

"I know that was hard, talking to him and telling him about Willow, but please take a moment to calm down. Don't speed when you drive out here. I'll get the kids when they get off the bus and wait for you to get home. Take your time. Everything is fine."

"Okay," Savvy said, disconnecting and tossing the phone back on the seat. But she didn't agree. She had three kids to raise. She had to fight the school to keep them from holding Dylan back. And she had to get over the knowledge that she wasn't the only wild child who had returned home.

Chapter Two

Brodie hit the brakes to keep from plowing into the back of Savvy's truck when she screeched to a stop at the intersection of Main and Maple. His mind reeled. He needed a moment to sort through the tornado of information he'd received, but he didn't have time to stop and process. He had to follow her, couldn't let her get away without telling him what had happened to Willow.

Willow. Dead.

After all this time, he was finally going to make things right, and she was dead?

God, why? And how?

That letter had been mailed less than a month ago. A month ago, she was alive. A month ago, he could have talked to her, helped her son the way she'd asked and apologized for treating her so badly.

Now that chance was gone.

He set his jaw and accelerated as Savvy continued out of town. She'd said she had to take care
of Willow's kids. Brodie had known Willow had
a son from that letter. How many more children
did she have? Had she been married? And if she
was, where was her husband?

And why was Savvy taking care of them now?

So many questions. And unfortunately, Savvy,
who could undoubtedly provide answers, didn't
want anything to do with him.

Brodie had been prepared to see Willow, but he
hadn't anticipated running into Savvy.

Savvy, still as stunning as ever, even in ratty
blue jeans, an old T-shirt and a baseball cap.
She'd been pretty in school, but she was down-
right gorgeous now. Hard to believe this was his
old friend. One of the two females he'd opened
up to in high school. In spite of the string of girls
he'd had physical relationships with back then,
Willow and Savvy were the only two that he'd
truly known. They'd been so close.

And he'd blown it.

Today, Savvy's dark eyes said it all. She hadn't
forgiven him for what he'd done to Willow. And
Brodie didn't blame her. He'd never said he was
sorry. He'd never asked for forgiveness. He'd
planned to do both today, but now that would
never be possible.

God, please, help me out here.

He'd only recently found a relationship with God, but he'd been talking to Him continually ever since he thought he might lose his daughter.

"I didn't get the chance to ask for Willow's forgiveness, but let Savvy forgive me, Lord. I know You sent me here for a reason, and if that's it, help me figure out how to make that happen."

Savvy couldn't stop thinking of Brodie as she drove her old truck down the once-familiar dirt road between Claremont and Stockville toward Willow's trailer. Gripping the steering wheel tighter, she forced herself to remember that day when Willow finally told her what Brodie had done. If she and Brodie were still friends, he could help her now. Comfort her in her loss. Tell her what to do about her new role as guardian of Willow's children.

But they weren't friends, not anymore. And Savvy had never felt the pain of that loss more than now.

What *was* she supposed to do with a teenager and six-year-old twins? She'd always adored Willow's kids, when they visited sporadically to take advantage of her proximity to the beach. But raising them? Savvy knew *nothing* about bringing up children, and she sure couldn't pull from her own childhood to know what to do. Her own mom had abandoned ship as soon as Savvy was born. What if Savvy inherited *her* motherly instincts?

Checking the mirror as she started up Willow's driveway, she saw that Brodie hadn't given up on his pursuit. Not that she had expected him to. Brodie Evans never backed down from a challenge.

As if knowing Savvy was near, Mandy walked around the side of Willow's ancient trailer. She had her brown hair pulled back in a low ponytail and wore a black sleeveless sweater, jeans and boots. Savvy thought of the clothes she'd brought from Florida. Not one sweater in the lot. She was as prepared for north Alabama weather as she was to take care of Dylan, Rose and Daisy.

Or as she was to take on the all-encompassing male bearing down on her truck.

"God, help me," she muttered, parking next to Willow's old baby-blue minivan and, frankly, feeling a bit surprised that she'd asked Him for help. She hadn't had anything to do with God since she'd left this town; why would He help her now?

He'd certainly never done anything to support her before.

Mandy neared the truck and gave Savvy a soft smile as she climbed out. Savvy hadn't been overly close to Mandy when they were in school, but she was the kind of girl everyone knew and liked. And Mandy hadn't dated anyone in high school, so Savvy had never gone after her boyfriend and attempted to break up their relationship.

The way she had for most every other girl at Claremont High.

She'd earned her reputation, that was for sure. And from the looks she received at the square today, the town hadn't forgotten. But thankfully, Mandy didn't let that stop her from offering friendship. Then again, her husband was the youth minister at the church, so maybe offering friendship to the wild child was a requirement.

In any case, Mandy and Willow had apparently become close, and Savvy was glad for that. Willow, like Savvy, didn't have many friends.

"Rose and Daisy are playing on the swing set with Kaden out back. I heard your truck," Mandy said, explaining why she'd walked to the front of the trailer and left the kids. Her son, Kaden, had been with her last night, too. He was eight, only two years older than the twins, but Rose and Daisy obviously looked up to the boy. Kaden had brought several books and read them stories before bed. It would have been nice if Dylan had wanted to read to his sisters, but he'd been in his room and had only come out to eat and shower.

"I appreciate you watching them until I could get here."

The slamming of another door and then heavy

footsteps behind her indicated Brodie had also exited his truck and now stood close enough that Savvy could feel solid, masculine warmth against her side.

"Brodie," Mandy said, directing her voice to that very spot and affirming Savvy's suspicion that he stood near, close enough to sense, and close enough to touch.

Savvy stuffed her hands in her pockets to keep from even accidentally touching the man who'd shattered her friend's heart.

"I tried to reach you last week to tell you about Willow," Mandy continued. "I called your office at the college, but I didn't get an answer, and I didn't feel it was the kind of message I should leave on your machine."

Brodie had undoubtedly been at the hospital in Knoxville when Mandy had called. "I appreciate you trying," he said, still shocked by the news of Willow's death.

"I remember how close the three of you were," Mandy remarked. "Y'all were practically inseparable when we were all in school."

Savvy coughed, and Brodie suspected it was fake, a way to get Mandy to stop talking so she could change the subject. They might have been apart for a decade and a half, but he still remembered Savvy's tactics. "You mentioned the girls are out back," she said, proving him right. "Where's Dylan? Is he inside?"

Mandy shook her head. "He's gone for a walk."

"By himself?"

Mandy smiled. "He's thirteen," she said simply.

"Right. Of course he can take a walk by himself. I'm going to have to remember that he's a teenager now."

Brodie thought about what she had ahead of her, raising a teenage boy. *Adolescence. Hormones. Anger. Girls.* She wouldn't like dealing with that last one, but even though it'd been twenty years, Brodie remembered what it felt like to be thirteen.

"Dylan had been having a difficult time before his mom died," Mandy explained. "Willow asked if Daniel could help him, since he's the youth minister at the church."

"Help him how?" Savvy asked.

"Tutoring him in school, primarily," Mandy said. "And also being there as a male figure in his life. He hasn't had anyone but Willow, since she didn't have a relationship with her parents anymore. No dad, no granddad in the picture. Kind of tough for a teenage boy."

Brodie cleared his throat. "She asked about me tutoring him, too," he said, pulling Willow's letter from his pocket. This time, he noticed Savvy staring at his address in Willow's swirling handwriting. "That's why I wanted to find her today, to let her know I wanted to help her son."

"You said you wanted to apologize," Savvy reminded him.

"I wanted to do that, too," he said, flexing his jaw.

Most people, particularly his athletes, were intimidated by his size, or his deep voice, or maybe even the way he looked at them.

But Savvy clearly wasn't intimidated. She was irritated. And Brodie suspected he knew why. She didn't like having him here, standing beside her, reminding her of the relationship that they'd once had and the way it had ended.

Because of him.

But Brodie had made a promise to God and to himself that he'd help Willow's son, and he wasn't going to break that promise. "I'm guessing Daniel is your husband," he said, refusing to look at Savvy and focusing totally on Mandy. "Is he going to tutor Dylan?"

"He told Willow he could help out, but he wasn't available as often as she wanted because of his obligations at the church," Mandy explained. "She wanted someone daily, or at least every other day. Willow had been trying to help Dylan and the girls herself, but she'd recently realized that they still weren't progressing quickly enough and that she needed help."

Brodie remembered Willow struggling in school. It hadn't come easy for her. Apparently, it didn't come easy for her children, either.

"Do you know of anyone who tutors daily around here?" Savvy asked her friend.

Mandy shook her head. "No." Then she looked to Brodie. "You said she contacted you about helping Dylan?"

"She wrote to me. I tried to call her and let her know I could tutor him, but I couldn't reach her. So I decided to come find her and let her know that I wanted to help." This time, before Savvy could prompt him, he added, "And I needed to apologize for treating her badly the last time I saw her."

He didn't miss the slight grunt from Savvy at his answer.

"Do you want me to ask around and see if I can find any tutors that could work with Dylan daily?" Mandy asked, looking at Savvy, but then adding to Brodie, "Or did you still want to work with him?"

"Yes, please ask," Savvy said, at the same moment that Brodie answered, "I want to work with him."

Mandy's eyebrows lifted. "Maybe y'all should talk about it and decide what you're going to do and then let me know."

"Would you check around, just in case that's

what I decide?" Savvy asked. "I was called in to meet with the principal today, and if Dylan doesn't pass the standardized tests next month, they're going to hold him back."

Savvy could only imagine how much worse Dylan's anger would be, how much further he would withdraw from the world, if he were removed from his friends.

She'd sure been angry.

Mandy shifted from one foot to the other. "He's gone through so much, maybe it would be good to hold him back a year."

"It wouldn't," Savvy said. "I know from experience."

Realization dawned on the young woman's features. "Oh, Savvy, I'm sorry. I knew that, but I forgot."

"It wasn't your fault. But that was sixth grade for me, so I was retained in elementary school when all of my friends moved to junior high. Dylan is in the eighth grade, so he'd be held back when all of his friends move to high school. Probably an even bigger deal than what happened to me." She shook her head. "I can't let them do that to him—I won't—so I've got to make sure he passes those tests."

Mandy wrapped both arms around Savvy so quickly that she nearly knocked her off balance.

"I'm glad the kids have you here. Willow obviously knew that you'd take good care of them." She squeezed firmly. "Daniel and I will pray for you and for Dylan's situation at school, and we'll try to find someone who tutors daily. Everything is going to work out," she said, holding on tight enough that Savvy's eyes watered.

Or that was what Savvy told herself. She wasn't crying because she missed Willow, or because she was now responsible for three young lives, or because she was back in the town that she'd told herself she hated. Besides, it wasn't the town that'd done her wrong, necessarily. But the church. And the man she'd met there who crushed her heart.

Mandy finally released her and brushed her own tears away. "Okay, then... Kaden and I need to get back home. I left Daniel watching baby Mia, and he's great with her, but he isn't all that keen on changing diapers."

"I'll stay out with the girls and let them play a little longer." Savvy glanced toward the wooded areas surrounding the trailer. "But how do I find Dylan?"

"He should come back on his own," Mandy said, a slight frown pulling at her lip. "I think he needs some help with his grief. He hasn't said a lot about the accident at Jasper Falls, but I know it was hard for him to leave her to go get help."

"Willow died at Jasper Falls?" Brodie's brusque

voice hinted that he felt the same way Savvy did about the last place their friend had been alive. The three of them had loved Jasper Falls. It'd been their safe haven when the world gave them grief, and the thought that Willow had died there didn't coincide with the blissful memories.

A pang of guilt stabbed Savvy. She'd merely blurted out that their friend had died without giving him any information. "Willow fell while hiking," she said. "Dylan was with her, and he went for help, but she didn't make it." That was all she knew, and it was enough.

His eyes filled with agony. "I can't believe..." He didn't finish the sentence.

"Should I go look for him?" Savvy asked Mandy.

"We've got another hour until dark. He'll come back," she said. "He's been doing this since the funeral. I think it's his way of coping. Maybe he's praying."

Savvy nodded, uncertain about whether it was smart to let an upset teenager roam the woods, but also uncertain about whether she knew what was smart or what wasn't regarding kids.

Before Mandy could go get them, Kaden rounded the corner of the trailer with Rose and Daisy at his heels.

"Who's that?" he asked, tilting his head toward Brodie.

"I'm Brodie Evans," he answered, offering Kaden a smile in spite of the fact that he still looked distraught over Willow. His dimples dipped with the action, and Savvy was reminded of the effect of a Brodie Evans smile.

She didn't want to be affected.

"You play baseball?" Kaden asked, pointing at his Stockville jacket, and then, after reading the embroidered name on the chest, he continued, "You're a coach? Seriously?"

"I am," Brodie said.

"I play baseball. I'll play coach pitch this year. Next year, I'll be in kid pitch league."

"That's great," Brodie said. "Maybe I can come see you play sometime, and then maybe you can come see my team play sometime at Stockville College."

"Cool!" Kaden said, then looked at Mandy. "Mom, I'm getting hungry, and they're hungry, too." The twins walked behind him wearing the identifying shirts Savvy had dressed them in this morning. Rose's pink T-shirt had a bright yellow *R* in the top left, and Daisy's yellow T-shirt had a pink *D*. Savvy needed the helpful identifiers, since she couldn't tell the two apart.

"Aunt Thavvy," Rose said, her missing front two teeth causing a precious lisp that made her seem even younger than six. Or maybe the girls seemed younger—smaller—because they'd lost their mama five days ago.

Savvy dropped to eye level with the girls. "Hey, Rose," she said as Rose moved into the crook of her right arm. "Hey there, Daisy," she said as Daisy found the left side.

Daisy hugged Savvy like Rose, but then pulled away, her green eyes blinking her eagerness to speak. "Aunt Savvy?" She had yet to lose those two teeth, which was good, since it provided another means for Savvy to tell them apart without asking.

"Yes, Daisy?"

"Mommy can't make us pancakes, or take us to church, or anything, since she's with Jesus now." Her small hand gripped the back of Savvy's shirt as she spoke, holding on as if she was afraid Savvy would slip away, too.

Savvy's stomach knotted. How could she give them everything they needed? She'd never been a mommy and didn't know all that much about it. But the girls were hurting, and Willow had apparently thought Savvy was the best person to take care of her kids in case something happened.

Willow, are you sure?

"Can you make pancaketh?" Rose asked.

"Yes," she answered. "I can make pancakes."

You're going to do fine, Mandy mouthed, and Savvy prayed that she was right.

After Mandy and Kaden left, Savvy turned to Brodie. "You should probably go, too."

"I want to meet Dylan," he said. "And I do want to help him, to tutor him the way Willow wanted."

Savvy figured as much, and those last four words—*the way Willow wanted*—were the ones that made her say, "You can meet him and see if he wants you to help him. But if he says no, then that's it. You'll go, and we'll get someone else to help—" She tried to sound authoritative, but her voice broke when a loud boom of thunder belted overhead.

"We'll see," Brodie answered, and then peered up at the charcoal clouds swiftly moving above the trees. "Storm is coming."

Rose and Daisy had already darted up the steps toward the trailer. "Hurry!" Daisy called. "We need to go in!"

"But whereth Dylan?" Rose asked.

"Go on inside," Savvy said, shivering as lightning sliced the sky. "Dylan will be here soon."

The girls disappeared into the trailer, and Savvy peered toward the woods, then yelped at a loud blast of thunder.

"Still scared of storms?" Brodie asked, the rumble of his voice resonating close to her left ear.

She nodded, too spooked to even attempt to lie. "But I'm also worried about Dylan." She looked at him, then back at the trailer. "I can't leave the girls, but…"

"I'll go find him," he said, before she'd even bolstered the courage to ask him for help. "You take care of the twins. I'll bring him back safely."

Lightning once again split the sky in two, and this time, it hit something with a deafening crack.

Savvy's hand flew to her throat as the rain began to fall.

"I'm pretty sure that hit a tree," he said. "Go back inside and get out of the storm. I'll find him. Don't worry."

But Savvy was worried. Because Dylan was lost, and because Willow had written to a guy she said she'd hate forever, and now Savvy relied on that very same guy…to find Willow's son.

Chapter Three

"Dylan! Dylan, can you hear me?" Brodie was glad he'd had the wherewithal to grab his jacket and flashlight out of his truck before heading into the woods. It'd gotten dark much quicker than he had anticipated, and the drizzling rain combined with the unseasonal wind chilled him to the bone. He hoped the boy had already made it home, but in case he hadn't, Brodie would keep looking.

When he was a teenager, he'd been familiar with this section of the woods that led to Lookout Mountain; however, he'd always entered from the Claremont side, near Landon Cutter's place. Coming in from the Stockville end was different. The trails weren't as wide and hadn't been cleared out. You could ride horses through the trails on the Cutters' property, and he'd often done that with his friends back in high school. Sometimes Landon and John Cutter would come along.

Sometimes Georgiana Sanders did, as well. But always Savvy and Willow.

They'd been the three "wild ones" of Claremont High back in the day. Always together, always defending each other to the end.

Willow, the one whose family expected perfection and who couldn't find her way out of her big brother's shadow. It hadn't surprised Brodie when Savvy said her son's name was Dylan. Naturally, Willow would continue idolizing her brother through her son. By the time Brodie, the army brat, had moved to Claremont in the ninth grade, he'd lived in more cities than he could count, thanks to his father's military career. But he'd found his comfort zone—and his baseball talent—in this town. Savvy, the self-professed black sheep of the Bowers family, abandoned by her mother as an infant and then raised by grandparents who loved her unconditionally but had no luck controlling her free spirit.

So much had changed since then, yet a lot had remained the same. Savvy. Just thinking of her now brought back so many feelings, so many untapped emotions. Her long, straight blond hair from high school had been cut into one of those modern styles that stopped just below the chin. She looked older, but not in a bad way. More mature. And those eyes were as dark as he remembered, except he'd never seen her give him the

look of venom he'd received today. She hadn't de-
nied that Willow had told her what happened way
back when. Brodie suspected fiery Savvy would
have a harder time forgiving him than Willow.

If either of them forgave him. Now he'd never
know if Willow did, but he still had a chance with
Savvy…after he found Willow's son.

A clump of wet pine sent him skidding toward a
thick tree trunk, and he grabbed a nearby branch
to keep from sliding down the mountain's incline.
It'd be easy to slip and fall on the loose leaves and
straw covering the ground, and he prayed Dylan
hadn't done just that. Or worse, slid off one of the
ledges that surrounded the summit.

God, please let him be safe, he prayed. And
then, thinking about what would come later, he
added, *And if it be Your will, let Savvy forgive me.*

He wiped thick, gummy sap from the tree
against the front of his jeans and continued to
plunge through the thick forest. "Dylan!" he
called again, yelling the name every ten feet or
so in case he'd gotten nearer to the boy. "Can you
hear me?"

A sound carried on the wind. It could've been
an animal, but Brodie didn't think so. He squinted
against the rain, now coming sideways and slap-
ping his face like needles.

"Dylan, is that you?" he yelled.

"Yeah!"

Brodie picked up his pace, sprinting toward the sound. He took another off-balanced slide when he hit a slick rock in the path. "Where are you?"

"Under the ledge!"

Pushing low limbs out of the way as he moved, Brodie quickly found the flat rock that crested Lookout Mountain's timberline. Several sections jutted out to form protrusions, and he now suspected Dylan had used one of those to take cover from the brunt of the storm. Smart kid. "Which one?" he called.

"Right here!" Dylan answered, sticking his head out of one of the shallow caves and looking up toward Brodie. Shielding his eyes from the rain, he asked warily, "Who are you?"

Brodie worked his way down the ledge to enter the small area with the boy. Dylan was taller and thinner than Brodie would've thought a thirteen-year-old would be, but Brodie didn't have a whole lot of experience with kids. Maybe this was the normal size of a boy that age. He'd only recently started mentoring teenagers in the Stockville area, and all of them had been sixteen-to eighteen-year-olds. Most of them were much bigger than this boy. Dylan looked kind of lanky, like a man who hadn't filled out yet. Which, Brodie realized, was exactly what he was.

"Hey, Dylan," he said, glad that the flat rock cut the wind so he could talk without yelling.

"I'm Brodie Evans. I'm a friend of your mom's and Savvy's."

The kid tilted his head, wet shaggy hair covering one eye before he slung it out of the way. "No, you're not." Before Brodie could explain, Dylan took a small step back. But even in the hint of retreat, he puffed his chest out, ready to fight if necessary.

The kid had guts, Brodie had to give him that. Then again, Willow had never been afraid of anything, either. But that was because she'd seen the worst of everything right inside her own home.

"I don't know you." That long hair completely covered Dylan's right eye, but the left one narrowed, plainly sizing up the enemy.

The woods were getting darker by the minute. Brodie needed to get him on the trail quick, while they could still find their way back. He held up his palms and said, "I know you don't. But your mom, Savvy and I were friends in high school."

The boy looked skeptical and backed up a little more, putting himself against the curve of the rock but squaring his shoulders with the move. If he thought he could outrun Brodie, he'd be sorely mistaken. However, he didn't want to get in a footrace with the kid, especially not on the side of a mountain covered with wet leaves and rocky terrain. No doubt, someone would get hurt. He needed to gain the boy's trust. Then Dylan shivered, and Brodie saw that his denim shirt and jeans were drenched, as were his boots.

He removed his jacket and held it toward the boy. "Here, it's waterproof and will help you stay warm until you can get home and put on dry clothes."

Dylan looked as though he would refuse the offering, but then his jaw tensed and he appeared to decide that the jacket would be a welcome addition on the long hike. He took it. "Thanks."

"You're welcome," Brodie said, already feeling the difference in the chill from removing the jacket and glad that the kid accepted it. The teenager would be lucky if he didn't get pneumonia from this escapade. Which made Brodie wonder why Dylan had been this far away from home. "Where were you hiking to anyway?" he asked.

Dylan slung the long hair away from his face. "Jasper Falls. I think I'm close, but the rain got too hard, and I couldn't tell where I was anymore." He spoke with confidence, even when admitting he'd gotten lost.

Jasper Falls, where Willow died. And from what Savvy had said, Dylan had been with her and had gone for help. "Why were you going there?"

"Because that's where she was alive." Dylan's words were mumbled this time, and he sounded every bit the little boy missing his mother and nowhere near man status. He looked away from Brodie as he spoke, his throat pulsing thickly from emotion. But Brodie heard.

Drawn to the teenager, he wanted to comfort him somehow, but Dylan was still pressed against the rock, his blue eyes darting from one patch of woods to another as though contemplating his getaway path.

God, let him trust me. And let me help him deal with the pain. Give me the right words.

Brodie cleared his throat. "I told Savvy that I'd try to find you. She's worried about you. I'm sure she's expecting me to bring you home. Do you think you can trust me to do that?"

"Why should I?" Dylan glared at him, and Brodie suspected he wasn't the first adult on the receiving end of that defiance. The kid looked as though he'd be right at home getting into trouble at school. Actually, he reminded Brodie of himself in that way. He had always itched for a confrontation with his teachers, his parents, pretty much anyone.

Dylan looked back to Brodie, and the wall that had surrounded him a moment ago slipped a bit. "Aunt Savvy is worried?"

Aunt Savvy. Brodie was touched that she had such a position in Willow's children's lives that they considered her an aunt. If he hadn't messed things up with Willow, he might have been Uncle Brodie. "Yeah."

Then Dylan's eyes widened, his attention captured by the embroidered emblem on Brodie's chest. "You're a coach? At the college?"

Finally, something that would break the ice with this kid. Same thing that had captured Kaden's interest earlier. "Yeah. The baseball coach. It's my first season there, but we're having a pretty good year. You play?"

Dylan shook his head. "I wanted to go out for the school team this year, but—" he shrugged "—I didn't."

Brodie waited to see if he'd say more, and his patience paid off.

"They cut a lot of kids," Dylan said.

Brodie understood the fear of not making the team. At thirteen, Dylan would try out for junior high, the first stage of athletics where the "everyone gets a trophy" approach flew out the window. He remembered it well. "Practice and determination, that's what'll get you on the team."

"Who would I practice with?" he asked, then flinched as though he wanted to take the words back. Probably hadn't planned on sharing that insight with a stranger.

"How about me?" Brodie wanted to help the boy deal with his loss, and if there was anything he knew, well, it was baseball. Plus, Willow's letter had insinuated that Brodie could help her son with tutoring. Maybe baseball would open that door, too. Something the boy wanted to do combined with something he needed to do.

"Why would you do that?" Dylan asked, clearly not used to adults offering to help him out.

Because I owe your mom. Because you remind me of myself. Because I need to right old wrongs to prove I deserve a spot in my daughter's life. "Because I love baseball," he replied.

"That'd be—" Dylan's jaw clenched as he apparently fought off a smile "—cool." Then his stomach growled loud enough to be heard over the wind. "I'm getting hungry." He held his hand out from the ledge. "The rain's slacking. Probably should go back."

So a promise of baseball practice and a hungry stomach caused him to think straight. Worked for Brodie. "Let's go."

Twenty minutes later, they exited the woods near the trailer with Brodie impressed at the boy's sense of direction. He'd led the way back and hadn't panicked when the rain picked up a couple of times or when he'd slipped on wet patches of leaves and pine straw. In fact, Dylan seemed very agile and easily adapted to his surroundings. Brodie suspected he'd probably be a decent baseball player.

He held the flashlight and shot the beam ahead

of them as they moved toward the trailer, where every floodlight gleamed and apparently every light inside also illuminated in anticipation of their arrival. They were still ten feet away when the door to the trailer opened and Savvy came out. Her relieved gasp reverberated as she darted into the rain. She threw her arms around Dylan in a tight bear hug that caused the boy to wince.

"Hey, Aunt Savvy, that's good," he said. "I'm okay."

"Thank God," she whispered, heavy tears falling freely.

The twins timidly stepped through the open doorway, but remained under the pitiful metal awning to stay out of the rain. They were identical, with fine blond hair surrounding cherubic faces, matching pink nightgowns and bare feet. "Dylan? You okay?" one asked.

He pushed away from Savvy and turned toward the girls. "I'm okay, Rose." Then he looked back at Savvy. "Sorry I was gone so long. Got caught in the rain."

She blinked, opened her mouth as though she wasn't certain how to answer, then responded, "That's okay, I guess."

He turned to Brodie and said, "You meant it about the baseball?"

"I did."

Dylan nodded, and this time released that hint

of a grin. "Okay, then." He jogged up the steps to the door and took the girls inside.

Savvy waited for the door to snap closed and then turned to Brodie. "What about baseball?" Her brow knitted, and she didn't make any effort to move toward the trailer, in spite of the fact that the rain still fell, and her T-shirt and jeans grew wetter by the minute.

"Don't you want to go inside and talk?" he asked.

"No." She shook her head, the ends of her hair converting from pale blond to caramel in the rain and then curling beneath her chin.

For some bizarre reason, Brodie wanted to touch the dampened hair, push it away from her face and see those dark eyes, try to find the pupils hidden within the irises.

"What did Dylan mean about baseball?" she asked, snapping him out of his reverie.

The rain picked up steam again, and he motioned toward the wooden deck that bordered the right half of the trailer. "I'll tell you, but let's at least get under the awning, if you won't let me come inside. You're getting drenched."

She glanced down, apparently realizing that her clothes were, in fact, soaked. "Okay, fine," she said. "But then you have to go." She started up the steps, then held up a palm. "Wait here." Then she went inside and left Brodie under the flat awning, which he now realized had a large hole in one side, where the rainwater streamed through.

She returned a moment later wearing a large camouflage jacket, probably Dylan's, over her shirt. When she opened the door, he heard the kids talking, and he tilted his head toward the sound. She pushed the door closed.

"Okay, tell me. What about baseball?"

"He wants to get better at baseball, and I offered to help."

A clap of thunder caused her to jump, and a yelp escaped that didn't go unnoticed by the kids, because the door opened and Dylan stuck his head out.

"Aunt Savvy, you okay?"

"Yes, Dylan, I'm fine," she said, but her voice quivered. "I made pancakes. There are some in the microwave for you."

Dylan's brow furrowed at Brodie, but then he looked to Savvy, who managed a smile in spite of the fact that Brodie knew she was terrified of this storm. In any case, the kid seemed appeased. "Okay. I'm going to eat. But let me know if you need me." He started inside, but then stopped and slid off Brodie's baseball jacket. "Thanks for letting me wear this."

"You're welcome." He took the coat and once again, found himself impressed. Barely a teenager, the boy was still ready to protect the women of his house.

When the door closed and the volume on the television promptly increased, Savvy gave him a pointed look. "I said you could see if he wanted you to tutor him, not teach him baseball. And I only mentioned that because that's what you said Willow wanted in that letter. If it isn't what Dylan wants, though, the deal is off."

"Willow wanted me to help him."

"So you say."

Brodie should've known she wouldn't take his word. He withdrew the letter and handed it over.

Savvy looked at the envelope, her lower lip rolling in as she ran a finger across the handwritten address on the outside. With shaky hands, she turned it over and withdrew the letter.

Brodie watched her eyes move across the page as she read each line. At the end, she closed her eyes, released a quivering breath and handed the letter back.

"Believe me now?" he asked.

She nodded. "But she only asked about tutoring. The baseball—"

"Will give me a way to break the ice by doing something he wants to do."

She mulled that over. "Okay. We'll try it. But if his grades don't get better, then no baseball or tutoring."

"He needs help. Willow said so, and you know it's true. Even more now that he's lost his mom."

"I know he does," she whispered, leaning her head toward the door to presumably make sure the kids were still listening to the television. "I'm just not so sure that help needs to come from you." Before he had a chance to argue, she added, "But I see that it's what Willow wanted, and I won't deny her request."

"Good," he said. "Because I do want to make things right. And whether you believe me or not, Savvy, I was going to tell her I was sorry and ask her to forgive me. Today. As soon as I saw her."

Savvy shook her head incredulously. "After all these years? You wanted to ask her forgiveness now?" She wrapped her arms around herself in an apparent effort to remain calm. "You never called to check on her. You never returned her calls, or mine, for that matter. You ignored emails. Dropped out of our lives altogether, as though *we'd* done something wrong. But you were the one…" Her voice quaked. "You ripped Willow's world apart. And mine." The last two words were spoken so softly that Brodie barely heard. But he did.

"I didn't call you because I knew she'd told you what I did, and I knew you wouldn't forgive me."

"You never really knew Willow, or you'd have

known she tried to protect you. She didn't want me to think badly of you. She *didn't* tell me."

"She— What?" Floored, Brodie tried to comprehend Savvy's words. He'd thought that Savvy would have been the first person Willow called after he left her in Knoxville. "Willow never told you?"

"Not for several years. When she and the kids would come visit at the beach, we'd always end up talking about you, about our friendship and about what we thought might have gone wrong. Why you stopped caring about the two of us."

Brodie flinched, the truth of her statement packing a powerful punch.

She shrugged. "Finally, she couldn't keep it from me anymore. She told me about the one-night stand, and the way you left her in the hotel in Knoxville. She'd thought your friendship had turned into love. Did you know that?"

She yanked the jacket tighter around her petite frame. "Did you ever think about what that night might have meant to someone like Willow? Someone who actually dreamed of the happily-ever-after that she'd never had in her own home? And that's what she thought she'd found—with you—until she woke up, and you were gone."

Brodie swallowed hard. "I messed up."

"Yeah, Brodie, you did. She ended up feeling like all of the other girls you left behind. And you did what you always did. You went on your merry way and never looked back. Not at Willow," she said, her words sharp and heated now, "or at me."

"Savvy, I can explain about what happened back then and why I left the way I did." He wanted to explain. *Needed* to explain.

The door cracked open, and Daisy peeked out. "Aunt Savvy, can we have dessert?"

She took a deep breath, exhaled thickly and then found a smile for the little girl. "Yes, there are some brownies on the counter."

Daisy's mouth slid to the side as she stared at Brodie, but she didn't ask why he was still there, wet and tired, standing in the rain. And wishing he could redo one day of his life. The night he'd crossed the boundaries of friendship with Willow…and the morning he'd abandoned her in that hotel room.

After the door closed, Savvy said, "I don't want to hear your explanation. No explanation would be sufficient for what you did. It's too late." She was so visibly mad that it wouldn't surprise Brodie if the rain came off her like steam. "You can help Dylan, because for some bizarre reason, that was one of Willow's last wishes." She shook her head in disgust. "I can't believe that the last letter she ever wrote…was to you."

Brodie started to clarify, to tell Savvy that the letter in his jacket probably wasn't the last one

Willow ever wrote, because this one had been penned almost a month ago. Obviously, since he'd just shown up today, Savvy assumed he'd received the letter very recently. If he told her the truth, she'd want to know why he hadn't come earlier. And, like his leaving Willow in that hotel room after a one-night stand, his explanation would fall short.

So he remained silent.

"I can come tomorrow, after Dylan gets out of school, if that'll work. I'll take him to the field and we'll hit a few. Then I'll talk to him about school."

A giant flash of lightning illuminated the sky and subsequently showcased the distress on her face at having to accept Brodie's offer. She jumped when the thunder that followed shook the trailer.

Brodie took a step toward her.

Savvy took a step back.

"I don't need you," she said fiercely.

He nodded. "I get that. But you used to."

Her eyes grew even darker. Did she also remember the many nights in high school when bad weather hit Claremont and she'd called Brodie? He'd either talk to her until the storm passed, or on a couple of occasions, he'd driven to her grandparents' home, met her on the front porch and held her while she cried.

"I don't need you," she repeated. "You left back then, and I haven't needed you since."

"You left first," he reminded her.

Savvy's chin quivered, and she shook her head so subtly that anyone else wouldn't have noticed. But Brodie did. She had left Claremont several months before he'd taken off for college. And she'd never looked back. Barely called Brodie and Willow for nearly three years, and neither of them knew why she'd headed south to Florida. He still didn't know. And she obviously wasn't telling.

"You can start working with Dylan tomorrow," she said, turning her back to him to enter the trailer. "But as soon as he passes those tests and gets approved to move on to ninth grade, you'll be done. And you'll stay away." Not bothering to wait for his response, she entered the trailer, closed the door and left Brodie standing in the rain.

Chapter Four

Savvy sat on the top step of Willow's wooden deck and reread the letter from the elementary school principal. She'd left the sporting-goods store at two to make certain to be here when the kids got home. It'd taken less than fifteen minutes, so she had time to get the mail.

And read this letter that stated the elementary school believed Rose and Daisy should be retained, too.

She was glad for the extra time, because she didn't want the kids around to hear her make this call. Pulling her cell from her pocket, she dialed the number on the letterhead. The bus wouldn't be here for another half hour. Surely this conversation wouldn't take that long.

"Claremont Elementary, how can I help you?"

After asking to be transferred to the head administrator, Savvy waited two hard heartbeats and then heard, "This is Principal Randolph."

She cleared her throat. "Hi, this is Savannah Bowers. I currently have guardianship of Willow—I mean Wendy—Jackson's children, and I received a letter from you today about Rose and Daisy."

Silence echoed from the other end, and then the woman said curtly, "And?"

Savvy hadn't expected the abrupt change of tone. Obviously, this lady didn't care for her, but Savvy didn't remember a soul in Claremont with the last name of Randolph.

She gathered her courage. "And," she continued, "the letter says that you're recommending Rose and Daisy be retained for a year, held back in first grade while their friends move on to second in the fall."

"That's correct," she said, her tone still terse. "The girls were already falling behind on their first-grade skills, and we believe, especially in light of their mother's recent passing, that it would be in their best interest to have the opportunity to repeat first grade."

"The *opportunity*," Savvy said.

"That's correct."

Savvy could feel her skin heating, readying for confrontation. She closed her eyes and counted to five. Ten was too much to ask for, given her frustration. "The letter says that I can come in and review their scores, and I can request for the girls to be reevaluated if I believe those scores may not be an accurate representation of their first-grade skills." Savvy read the text verbatim from the woman's letter.

"That's correct. However, in my opinion—"

"I'd like to make an appointment to do that," Savvy said, hearing a vehicle coming up the driveway. Mandy had told her the bus dropped the kids off at the end of the driveway and then they walked the rest of the way. Plus, it still wasn't time for the bus. She frowned as Brodie's truck appeared through the trees bordering the driveway.

Great...just great. Now I have to deal with him on my own until the kids get home.

"You'd like to make an appointment?" the lady on the other end asked, reminding Savvy she was still on the phone.

"Yes, an appointment," Savvy said hastily. "I do have the right to do that, don't I? I am their legal guardian now."

The lady actually huffed on the other end. "Yes," she said. "You can make an appointment. When would you like to come?"

"As soon as possible. Tomorrow, if that works for you."

"Well, I am busy." She drew out the last word.

"Then I'll wait until the end of the day, when school is over, and we can meet then," Savvy answered.

Another huff filled the line, followed by a low grumble. What did this woman have against Savvy? They'd never even met. Or maybe she had something against Willow?

"You can come at nine in the morning," she said. "But I don't anticipate any change to our original observations. I've reviewed the progress reports from their teacher, and given—"

"I'll see you at nine," Savvy said, cutting her off and ending the call without saying goodbye. In other words, she hung up on the lady, which suited her just fine.

"Someone on your bad side?" Brodie asked, sauntering toward the deck. He wore a Stockville College baseball jersey, baseball pants and a matching cap.

"You mean besides you?" She hated that the look of him in that baseball uniform made her heart thud in her chest.

He had the nerve to grin, and then he held up his palms. "I understand that you're mad at me, but I think, for Dylan's sake, it'd be good for us to get along in front of him. If he can tell that you don't like me, it isn't going to make it easy for him to like me, either."

"I *don't* like you," Savvy said.

"I get it. But if we can try to coexist so that I have a chance to help Willow's son, then we'll accomplish what *she* wanted." He sighed. "I've been thinking about this all day, Savvy, and I want this chance to help Dylan. I need it."

She looked down at the paper still in her hand. Somehow she had to make sure the school didn't hold these kids back. And Brodie was probably her best shot at doing that for Dylan. "I told you that you could tutor him, if it's what he wants."

"It will be." He'd moved closer to the steps so that he merely had to lean forward to peer over her shoulder and see the letter. "What's that?"

Savvy didn't see any reason not to tell him. "The elementary school thinks the girls should be held back, too. I've got to go talk to the principal tomorrow to convince her that isn't what they need." She looked at the letterhead, saw the woman's name beneath the address. "This says her name is M. Randolph. Did we know any Randolphs in school?"

"Not that I recall."

"That's what I thought."

"So do you think you can change this Principal Randolph's mind?"

"I'm not sure." Savvy bit her lip, still trying to place the name and coming up with nothing.

"Well, as a preemptive strike, do you want me to tutor the girls, too?" Brodie asked.

Savvy glanced up, saw the sincerity in his eyes and knew he meant the offer. But Willow hadn't asked him to help the girls, and truthfully, Savvy didn't want him around any more than necessary. "No, I'll figure something out. You help Dylan. That's plenty." She glanced at her phone and saw that it was only 2:25 p.m. She'd have to spend twenty more minutes alone with Brodie before the bus arrived.

As if knowing her train of thought, he said, "I didn't have your number to call and see what time the kids got home, and I wanted as much time with Dylan as possible before my team's evening practice at seven. Guess I got here a little early."

"They should be here at two forty-five."

He moved in front of the steps, pointed to the spot next to Savvy. "Mind if I sit down while we wait?"

She did mind, but she couldn't think of a good reason to tell him why, so she shrugged. "Go ahead."

He filled the remainder of the wooden step, and Savvy edged over to put the hint of a distance between them. It was bad enough that she caught herself inhaling the combined scent of aftershave and soap, or whatever it was that created a spicy, masculine aroma that surrounded the man. To find herself leaning into the warmth of him sitting next to her would not be acceptable. She didn't want to enjoy his presence, and she wouldn't.

As long as she didn't scoot in his direction.

The wooden step creaked in protest as he shifted his weight to turn and view the front of the trailer. Savvy wasn't all that certain the thing would keep holding them up. The warped stairs were in as dire shape as the rest of the home. "This place is in rough shape, isn't it?" he said, as if reading her thoughts.

"Yeah." Yesterday had been overcast and stormy, and she hadn't been able to truly view the state of Willow's home. Today, however, in the clear afternoon, she observed the siding peeling away from the ends of the trailer, the holes in the awning where the rain had poured through, the rotted wood flaking away on the handrails and the misshapen stairs. And then there were the gaping holes in the skirting, big enough for a medium-size animal to slide between. She did *not* want to think about what might be living beneath the trailer.

"What made you decide to stay here, instead of taking the kids with you back to Florida? I'm guessing you were still living there?"

The thought had crossed her mind, several times, in fact. But she couldn't do that to Dylan, Daisy and Rose. "I was, but I didn't want to pull the kids away from their home, out of their school, away from friends and all of that."

Still eyeing the pitiful trailer, he asked, "But why stay here? Why not move into your grand-parents' place by the fishing hole? They've got plenty of space, don't they?"

Savvy nodded. "Yeah, and they offered, but this is where Willow raised her children. And she tried her best to make it a home." She pointed to the row of bright yellow flowers lined up like sturdy soldiers across the front of the trailer, as though protecting everyone who lived inside. "I imagine when she planted those daffodils, she wanted to make sure the place had a happy color visible every spring."

"Willow always liked flowers," he said.

Savvy thought about the white-and-yellow daisy necklaces she and Willow had made on the school playground during that sixth-grade year, when Savvy had been so sad at being held back and Willow had become the friend she needed. Willow had provided the color Savvy so des-perately needed in her dismal world. Then she thought of the other ways Willow had attempted to beautify this place.

"And those metal sunflowers hanging from the awning, and the flowerpots on both sides of the door. Willow tried her best to make this a nice home for the kids, and this is the only home they've known. I couldn't make them move away from here, not after all they've been through."

"You really do relate to them," he said quietly.

Drawing a deep breath, Savvy felt her pent-up emotions pushing through each word, and she didn't hold them back. "It's hard enough losing a mom who never really was a parent. I can't imagine how hard it is for them losing Willow. She was a good mom. And I don't want them to feel like they're being punished because their mama died."

"The way you felt."

It wasn't a question, so Savvy didn't answer. She simply nodded.

"That's why you're so determined to make sure the kids aren't held back. You don't want their lives turned upside down any more than necessary after losing their mom. And you know what that's like."

"Yeah," she said. "I do."

"And you want to stay here, in the only home they've known, because this is where they knew a sense of family," he continued.

Again, Savvy nodded. "When she was pregnant with Rose and Daisy, she told me that her boyfriend—their dad—was going to build her dream house after they married."

"What happened?" Brodie asked.

"They weren't married when she had the twins, but they had planned a wedding that next summer.

Then he died in a car wreck before they married. And Willow was left with the three kids to raise on her own." Savvy took a breath, let it out. "She never loved anyone else."

"What about Dylan's dad?" Brodie asked.

"He was never in the picture." Savvy didn't want to add that Willow had turned from one guy to another after high school, when she wanted so desperately to be loved. Every time Savvy called her from Florida, she'd be dating someone new and had always been certain she'd met *the one*. "And I feel bad now that I didn't realize how alone she was here. I thought I was doing a good thing, having her and the kids come down and visit me every year and spend time on the beach. But I should've come back to visit her some, too. Then maybe I could've helped."

"You're helping her now," he said softly. "Taking care of her children and looking out for their best interest, too."

Savvy smirked. "Those are the words both of the principals used. *Looking out for their best interest*. In their opinion, holding the kids back *is* looking out for their best interest."

"If anyone knows that isn't true, it's you."

"I remember that day like it was yesterday, when I learned about mom." Savvy thought back to when she came home from school to find her grandmother crying. "But you know what was the strangest part about it all, when I learned that she'd died?"

"Tell me," he said, in almost the exact same tone he'd used when they were in school. The one that said he was willing to listen, and that he cared.

"It was that I looked forward to them bringing her body home. So that I could finally see her." She swallowed, remembered seeing her mother for the first time and wishing that she would open her eyes so Savvy could see if they looked like hers. "That was the first time, the only time, that I ever saw my mom. And she was in a coffin."

Brodie slid across the step, wrapped an arm around her in much the same way he had done when they were teenagers. "I'm sorry you had to go through that."

"She died in April, like Willow, when the school year was nearly over. And so they held me back, because it was in my best interest." She placed her fingers against her forehead and rubbed them back and forth to relieve the tension that formed whenever she thought about that painful year. "I can't let Willow's children go through that."

"I know you won't," he said. "And I'll do anything I can to keep that from happening, too." His fingers caressed the top of her left arm, not in an intimate gesture but as a sign of a comforting friend.

Savvy did feel comforted, until the brakes from the school bus screeched and she realized the kids would soon amble up the driveway. And it suddenly dawned on her that she had succumbed to the charm of Brodie Evans once more.

She didn't need comfort from the guy who'd treated Willow so terribly.

Clearing her throat, she shifted to remove herself from the warmth of his arm and force his hand away.

Brodie heard the bus brakes at the same time as Savvy, and he knew the exact moment when she realized she was talking to him again, opening up to him. She moved away, and the air between them transitioned from the warmth of old friends to frigid and bitter strangers.

God, help me build her trust in me again. Help me do the right thing, not only for Savvy, but for Willow and her children.

The girls emerged through the tree-lined driveway first, and their eyes visibly brightened when they viewed Savvy and Brodie waiting on the steps. Both of them increased their pace, pink-and-purple book bags bouncing against their backs as they hurried across the dirt-laden yard.

"Aunt Thavvy, Daisy had to move a thtick," Rose said as she approached the deck.

Daisy, who'd been jogging to catch up with her sister, slowed to a crawl. "I didn't mean to."

Savvy scooted to the bottom step, held out an arm for Rose to curl inside and then held the other out for Daisy. But the second little girl had stopped walking.

"Daisy had to move a stick?" Savvy questioned.

Rose nodded solemnly. "Yes."

Savvy looked from the girls to Brodie, and he could see the confusion on her face. She mouthed, *Do you know what that means?* and he lifted his shoulders and shook his head in a "no clue" gesture.

One corner of Savvy's mouth dipped, and then she turned back to the girls. "And why do people have to move sticks?"

"Becauth they are bad," Rose said.

Savvy's eyebrows lifted at that. "Daisy, were you bad?"

"I guess so," the little girl replied.

Savvy looked to Brodie again, and once more, he gave her nothing. He had no idea what you did with kids either, and certainly couldn't offer any suggestions. So she returned her attention to Daisy. "How were you bad? What did you do?"

"I threw dirt in Justin's face," she said.

Brodie watched Savvy inhale, her head tilting

as though she were deciding what to ask next. And she asked what he'd have asked.

"Why did you throw dirt in his face?"

"Because he said I couldn't plant a flower with everybody else," Daisy said.

Savvy had been leaning toward the girls, but she straightened and glanced at Brodie.

He took that as his turn to jump in. "Why did Justin say that?" he asked.

"Because the flowers are for mommies, and he said I don't have one anymore."

"Tho Daisy threw dirt at him," Rose said. "And moved her thtick." She looked at her sister. "Ith Daisy in trouble?"

"No," Savvy said firmly. "No, she isn't. Daisy, did the teacher ask why you threw dirt at Justin?"

Daisy shook her head, her eyes blinking several times to apparently hold back tears.

"Daisy, I'm coming to the school in the morning, and I'll explain why you were upset with Justin."

Brodie watched Dylan approach, his head looking at the ground as he trudged along, kicking a rock in his path. Apparently, Daisy wasn't the only one who'd had a bad day.

"Justin shouldn't have said that," Savvy continued, paying more attention to the child in front of her than the teenager moping along the driveway, "but next time, when someone says something that upsets you, you shouldn't throw dirt in his face. You should tell the teacher and let her handle it."

"Then Justin would move a stick?" Daisy asked.

Savvy nodded. "I would think so."

"Mine just moved from green to yellow," Daisy explained. "That's a warning. You get a warning before your stick goes to red. When it goes to red, you get time-out at school."

"And no TV at home," Rose added.

Savvy turned to Daisy. "Well, I'm thinking we may not even have to worry about sticks moving again, because you won't be throwing any more dirt in Justin's face, right?"

The little girl nodded. "Right." She waited a beat, then asked, "Aunt Savvy?"

"Yes?"

"Can I still plant a flower for Mommy?"

Brodie tried to tamp down the surge of sadness rushing through him at her request. He was impressed that Savvy found the ability to talk without her voice breaking, because he wasn't sure he could do the same.

"Yes, Daisy, you can still plant a flower for her," Savvy said softly. Then she gave the girls a hug while Dylan apparently noticed Brodie on the porch and forgot about the rock in his path.

"Are we practicing baseball?" he asked, his entire disposition lifting with the question.

"That's why I'm here," Brodie replied.

Savvy shot him a look that told him he'd better cover why he was really here, and so he obliged.

"And I thought we might talk about your schoolwork, too."

Dylan stopped his progression toward the porch. "My schoolwork?"

Brodie could feel more than see Savvy's anticipation for his answer. But he'd prayed about this all day, and he knew God would help him say the right thing. "If it's okay with you, I'd like to help you practice baseball one day, and then help you with your school assignments the next."

"But you're a baseball coach," Dylan said.

Brodie heard Savvy's muffled laugh at his response. Did the kid think baseball coaches only knew anything about baseball? But instead of stating that he'd actually completed his bachelor's degree in sports management, Brodie explained, "I am a baseball coach, but I also help teenagers with their school assignments."

"Like a tutor or something?" Dylan asked with a scowl.

"You could call it that," Brodie said, "but you could also say I like to mix both kinds of learning when I teach someone about baseball."

Brodie sat on the step above Savvy now, and

she turned to look up at him. He noticed that her eyes looked like melted chocolate in the afternoon sunlight.

"Two kinds of learning?" Dylan asked, and Brodie took his attention away from shades of chocolate to the boy standing in front of him.

"Physical and mental. They go together, you know. A baseball player—a good baseball player—can't merely know how to play the game. He's got to be able to think, to analyze the play and what should be done in any situation."

"Like if you've got three balls and one strike, then you swing only at hitter's pitches," Dylan said.

Brodie grinned—he couldn't help it. He'd seen yesterday in the storm that the kid had survival skills, but he also had baseball knowledge too. "Exactly."

"I like to read sports books," Dylan admitted. "I just don't like to read schoolbooks so much."

"I remember the feeling," Brodie said. "But I can promise you, you'll go further in life, and even in baseball, if you learn both."

Dylan had been carrying his backpack, and he slung it on his shoulder. "I don't have any homework or anything tonight."

"Okay, then, why don't we go to Hydrangea Park and practice throwing?" Brodie asked.

Both of the girls were still in the crook of

Savvy's arms, but they wiggled out and looked his way.

"Can we go to the park, too?" Rose asked.

"And play on the merry-go-round and the slide?" Daisy added. Then, realizing they were asking the wrong person, she turned to Savvy. "Can we, Aunt Savvy? Please? I promise I'll try not to move my stick again this week. Or ever."

Brodie looked to Savvy. "What do you say, Sav?"

"I don't see how I can say no."

Three hours later, Brodie pulled into the same spot in Savvy's driveway with three sweaty kids chattering in the extended cab of his truck and Savvy sitting on the front passenger's seat. Dylan, as he suspected, had some baseball talent, and Brodie was pretty sure they'd only tapped the surface today with their friendly game of catch.

Rose and Daisy had kept Savvy busy on the playground that centered the ball fields, and Brodie had enjoyed watching the girls—and Savvy—have a good time in spite of the sadness that had surrounded them over the past week. Brodie had been enjoying himself so much that he'd nearly stayed too long, but he still had an hour before his team practiced, and the drive to Stockville wouldn't take him more than twenty minutes tops.

No, he wouldn't have time to grab something

to eat, but that was okay. He could eat later. And he'd spent his afternoon doing exactly what he needed to do. He could feel it to his core.

Thanks, God.

"You said a day of baseball and then a day of school," Dylan said, climbing out of the truck. "Does that mean we'll do schoolwork tomorrow?"

"That's right," Brodie said.

"I guess if we have to," Dylan grumbled. "But then we'll do baseball again, right?"

"That's a promise. You've got too much talent not to perfect it."

Dylan's face lit up. "Seriously?"

Brodie had encouraged the kid all afternoon, but he must not have realized he meant it. "Seriously."

Dylan didn't hold back his grin as he reached for Rose and helped her out, and then did the same for Daisy. And again, the boy impressed Brodie. "All right, then," he said, closing the door and starting toward the trailer with Daisy and Rose on each side.

Savvy watched them leave and reached for the door handle as though she weren't going to tell him goodbye. Then she paused and glanced over her shoulder.

"I appreciate what you're doing for him," she said quietly.

"I want to do it."

She nodded, got out of the truck and closed the door.

Brodie needed to get on the road, but he watched until she climbed the porch steps and paused near the door. He waited, wondering if she'd wave, or smile, or anything.

She entered the trailer without looking back.

Chapter Five

"Can you check again?" Savvy asked Principal Randolph's assistant.

The young girl, who couldn't be more than twenty-two, looked at her the same way she had for the past hour and fifteen minutes. With pity. Even she knew that the woman on the other side of that door was being rude. Mean, even. Savvy had arrived promptly at eight forty-five in case she was called in early, and she'd sat in this uncomfortable chair ever since while at least three other people gave their names and breezed right in. And out.

"I have checked, Ms. Bowers, each time you've asked, and Principal Randolph hasn't been available to see you yet. I do apologize."

Savvy had no doubt the girl was indeed sorry, but that didn't stop Savvy from growing more irritated by the minute. And she refused to leave without seeing the principal. "Would you mind checking again?" Savvy asked, as politely as she could manage.

The girl—Allison Brooks—based on her nameplate, said, "Sure, I'll ask again." Then she moved to the door, tapped on it and slid inside.

While Savvy waited.

A few minutes ticked by, then Allison returned and nodded. "She'll see you now."

"Hallelujah," Savvy said, but anxiety shivered down her spine. Why didn't the woman want to talk to her? And why did Savvy dread this visit to the principal's office almost as much as the visits she'd endured throughout middle and high school?

Allison held the door open for Savvy, then closed it after she'd passed through, giving Savvy the opportunity to finally see the woman who'd been abrupt on the phone and disrespectful this morning.

Though the face had aged, Savvy recognized it. "Micca? Micca Landry?"

Deep auburn eyebrows rose to disappear beneath the same color bangs. "Monica," she corrected. "And my last name is Randolph now, Savvy."

"Right, Monica," Savvy said, her stomach pitching at the last memory she had of Micca, outside the Claremont High gym on prom night. One hand covering her mouth as she cried, and the other hand cradling her stomach as though she might throw up. Because of Savvy. "I, well, you went by Micca in school. So…"

"I've been Monica since college," she said, curt tone returning. "We all grow up." Then she scanned Savvy from head to toe, surveying her fitted maroon T-shirt, skinny jeans and boots with unhidden disdain. "Some of us do anyway."

Savvy tamped down the sassy reply that beckoned to be shared and instead motioned to one of the visitor chairs in the office. "Should I sit here?"

Micca—Monica—nodded and reached for two manila folders at the side of her desk. Savvy saw *Rose Jenkins* and *Daisy Jenkins* written across the tabs.

How could life be so cruel that Rose and Daisy's fate would be determined by someone Savvy had treated so badly?

"Micca," Savvy started.

"Principal Randolph," she corrected, pushing multicolored reading glasses up the bridge of her nose as she flipped Rose's file open.

"Sorry, Principal Randolph," Savvy said. "I wanted to talk to you about the recommendation you made to hold the girls back. From someone who has been through that in the past, I would ask you to reevaluate them before keeping them from their friends and making them repeat the work they've already done." She'd been practicing this speech all morning, and it sounded pretty good, if it weren't for the fact that this woman clearly despised her.

Micca released the top of the folder and let it drop closed. "I remember when you were held back, Savvy. That put you in the same grade as me."

Savvy hadn't thought about that. She had graduated with Micca, but they hadn't originally been in the same grade. That repeat of sixth grade had put the two of them together, which meant that this lady was a year younger than Savvy. Thirty-two. She looked so much older, with that same bobbed hairstyle she'd worn back in high school and thick turquoise eyeliner shading both eyes. And her skin looked dull, as though she could use a good facial...

Micca's glasses slid down, and she peered over them at Savvy. "*What* are you doing?"

Savvy had been examining the woman and determining all of the ways Micca could make herself look better; in other words, looking at Micca the same way she'd always looked at her in school. Micca could've been a pretty girl, but she tried too hard, and the results were, in Savvy's opinion, a complete failure. But Micca did get a prom date with that cute guy from Stockville, the one she'd met at a church camp during spring break.

And Savvy'd had to go and sabotage that.

Micca leaned over the desk, lowered her voice

and said, "Before you say something you may regret, Savvy, I should remind you that *I* am the one in control now. This isn't high school, and you won't always get what you want. Understand?"

Ouch. Savvy, again, remembered how she'd hurt Micca, and she didn't blame her for being mean. In fact, she admired the girl for gaining a backbone with age. "Yes, I understand. And I do care about what's best for the girls, and for Dylan, too, and I can't believe holding them back will do anything but harm them." The sincerity in Savvy's voice surprised her, but she meant every word, and from the way Micca studied her now, the principal might believe she meant them, too.

"I've never punished a child because of his or her parents—or their guardian, in this case—and I won't now," Micca stated firmly.

"I appreciate that," Savvy replied, "more than you know."

"But—" she flipped Daisy's file open and then followed suit with Rose's "—both of the girls are behind, primarily in their reading skills. They are both well below grade standards, and from the midyear tests performed after the Christmas break, they are still struggling with even the simplest necessities."

"Such as?" Savvy asked.

"Their sight words. Both Rose and Daisy failed their tests on basic sight words midway through the year. If they can't read, they cannot be pro-moted. They should be reading simple sentences now, not struggling on the sight words they should've mastered in kindergarten."

Savvy nodded. "So we'll work on that. On their reading, and especially sight words. Then when can they be tested again?"

Micca frowned.

"Your letter said they could be tested again if I disagreed with the evaluation, and I do."

Micca closed the folders. "They can be tested again in May, when we administer the standard-ized achievement tests."

"And if they pass?"

"It's highly unlikely that they—"

"But if they do, they can advance to second grade, right?"

"Savvy, the girls have been through a lot. They've never had a father."

"They did," Savvy corrected. "He would've been around, too, but he died before he and Wil-low were married."

"Okay, but the truth stands that for the major-ity of their life, they haven't had a father, and now they've lost their mother, and to be completely honest, they weren't doing all that well before Willow passed away. And just today, I received a notice from Mrs. Carter that Daisy was involved in an altercation with a young boy yesterday."

"Are you talking about her throwing dirt in Justin's face?" Savvy asked.

Micca opened Daisy's file and lifted a square pink slip. She scanned the comments and nodded. "Yes, that's what was reported by Mrs. Carter, her teacher."

"Does it say *why* she threw dirt in his face?"

Still looking at the paper, Micca shook her head. "No, it doesn't."

She quickly filled Micca in on what exactly had transpired between Justin and Daisy, then watched as Micca's mouth flattened.

"I see," the principal said. "The children are beginning their Mother's Day projects, and I'm sure Mrs. Carter didn't realize that was the reasoning behind the act."

"It'd be nice if she took that into consideration, particularly with them discussing Mother's Day, since that's going to be a tough holiday at our home." Savvy felt odd calling Willow's trailer her home. But right now that was exactly how it felt. Like her home.

"I'll speak to Mrs. Carter about it," Micca assured her.

"I appreciate that," Savvy said. "And just to clarify, if the girls pass that test in May, they can be promoted?"

Micca placed her hands flat on the girls' files. "And as *I* tried to mention before, the likelihood of them passing with their scores currently so low is very slim."

"That doesn't answer my question."

Micca sighed loudly. "If they were to pass, then yes, they would advance to second grade."

Savvy stood. "That's all I needed to know. Thank you for meeting with me." She held out a hand, because it seemed the right thing to do.

Micca stared at the offering for a moment, then also stood and placed her hand in Savvy's. "I'm doing it for the girls, Savvy. Not for you."

They shook hands, and Savvy turned to go, but then she stopped and pivoted toward the desk. "Micca."

"Principal Randolph," she said authoritatively.

Savvy nodded. "Fine. Principal Randolph, I need to…say something to you."

"I would've thought you said all you needed to say."

It'd be easy for Savvy to agree and then leave, but it wouldn't make her feel any better about how she'd done this woman wrong so long ago. "I need to say—" she gathered the words "—that I'm sorry."

The arched eyebrows rose again, causing the glasses to slide to the tip of her nose. "You're sorry?"

"For what happened on prom night. I could

tell, I mean, everyone knew that you really liked that guy."

"His name was Vic," Micca huffed.

"Right. Vic." Savvy hadn't even remembered his name. "And I shouldn't have, well, if I could do it again, I wouldn't have…"

"Flirted with the only guy I'd ever cared about, the only one who mattered to me up to that point, and then convinced him to leave the prom—my senior prom—with you instead of taking me home?"

Savvy had gotten angry with her own date and decided to hurt him by leaving with someone else. The problem had occurred when the cute stranger she'd started talking to had actually come to the prom with Micca. "Yeah, I'm very sorry for that," Savvy said before turning and leaving Micca's office.

And with each step out of the school and to her truck, Savvy thought of the mistakes she'd made and all of the people she'd hurt in the process. And then she thought of others who'd made past mistakes and might also be sorry. One person in particular.

Brodie.

Chapter Six

Brodie had gone thirteen years without knowing anything about his daughter, but ever since that trip to the hospital, he hadn't stopped thinking about her, wondering how she was doing and whether she ever thought of him. Before giving himself a chance to second-guess the impulse, he picked up the phone and dialed Cherie's number.

It rang three times. He imagined her staring at the display on her cell, realizing it was him and then ignoring the call. So he wasn't expecting the click identifying an answer on the other end.

"Brodie," she said, skipping past hello. "You shouldn't be calling me."

He took a breath, let it out. She was right, of course. She was his ex-wife, married to a man who obviously loved her and his daughter very much. But that daughter was Brodie's first, and she'd been hurt. "I wanted—needed—to know how Marissa is doing. How's her leg?"

Cherie's sigh echoed through the line. "It's healing well. Physical therapy is going great. She's determined not to miss any more softball than necessary, so she's working hard." She paused. "But you shouldn't be calling, Brodie. I told you at the hospital, I wouldn't ever have called you if I hadn't thought that she wasn't going to make it. And even then, it was Ryan's idea."

Brodie had learned at the hospital that it'd been Cherie's husband who'd thought they should let Brodie know Marissa had been in the accident. And Brodie's opinion of the guy had skyrocketed with that realization. Surely Ryan would know then that Brodie would also want an update on Marissa's healing. And maybe he'd even understand that Brodie wanted some kind of small place in her world. "I've been worried about her," he said. "I just wanted to know how she was doing."

"She's fine."

"Cherie, I meant what I said at the hospital. I want to change, be a better person. And I want to have a place in my daughter's life, if you and Ryan will let me."

"Brodie, honestly, what makes you think Marissa would even want you to have a place in her life now? You left when she was just a baby."

The truth of her statement stung to his core, but Brodie wouldn't believe that he hadn't been brought back into her life for a reason. "Cherie, I'm getting my life right with God, and I've been helping the son of a friend who passed away. I've started realizing the things that matter."

He waited, expecting her to say something like "It's about time," but she surprised him when she whispered, "I'm glad for you, Brodie. I really am. But that doesn't mean Marissa would welcome you into her life with open arms. Surely you realize that."

"Will you tell her I called to check on her?"

"She's at school."

"When she gets home," he said, and also said a silent prayer that Cherie would grant him this request.

The silence from the other end warned him that he was about to be disappointed, but again, Cherie surprised him.

"I'll tell her," she said. "Goodbye, Brodie." Then she disconnected, and Brodie said another silent prayer, this one thanking God for her saying yes.

He'd planned on waiting until school ended before he drove to Willow's place to work with Dylan. But he'd already conducted the morning workouts, answered necessary emails and made that call to Cherie, and now he found himself studying the clock and counting the hours until he saw Savvy and the kids again.

He'd prayed for God to show him what he needed to do to earn a place in his daughter's world, and he knew God had brought him here, to Stockville, near Savvy, because he was meant to help her with the kids. Maybe that was why he left his office at a quarter till noon and headed toward Claremont.

At ten past twelve, he entered the sporting-goods store and decided God had sent him there for a reason, too. Because if he hadn't stepped through that door at precisely that moment, he might not have caught his pretty blond friend as she fell from the top of a six-foot ladder.

One minute he was contemplating what he'd say when he saw her, and the next minute he caught her in his arms, her soft hair tickling his chin as she twisted to face him, dark eyes wide with shock and disbelief. "You always attack customers when they enter the place?" he murmured.

"Yeah," she whispered, then blinked and shook her head. "Um, no. I mean, no."

"Savvy! Oh, honey, I'm so sorry. I went to the back to get the netting for that display and didn't think about you climbing to the top of that ladder," her grandmother said, hurrying toward them. "Brodie, I'm so glad you caught her!"

"No problem at all," he said, bouncing her in

his arms before adding, "She never weighed a whole lot. Lucky for me, that hasn't changed." He grinned and waited for some feisty reply, but Savvy seemed at a loss for words.

So he kept her there, in his arms. He certainly didn't mind it, and who knew? Maybe she was still in a bit of shock and needed to be held.

Or maybe Brodie wasn't ready to put her down quite yet.

"Dear, are you hurt?" her grandmother asked, probably because Savvy *hadn't* made an effort to get down, and Brodie hadn't made any effort to free her.

Apparently snapping back to the here and now, Savvy wiggled in his arms. "No, I'm fine. Brodie, can you put me down, please?"

He nodded and then naturally guided her to the floor. He'd said the truth; she still didn't weigh a whole lot, probably not much more than in high school. But as many times as he had comforted her back then, he couldn't recall a single time that he'd held her in his arms like just now.

"Thanks for catching me," she said, refusing to look at him, which reminded him that she was still mad at him for what had happened in the past. It also reminded him of why he came here today—to try to gain her trust once more so he could finally make amends.

"You're welcome," he said.

Savvy's grandmother tilted her head, pursed her lips and glanced from Brodie to Savvy and back again. Then her mouth curved into a smile. Brodie had no idea what Jolaine Bowers was about to say, but Savvy didn't give her a chance to get started.

"I'll get the rest of the items for the display from the back of the store. Brodie, I'm sure my grandmother can help you with whatever you need." She took a step toward the aisle, leading to her exit, or so she thought.

Brodie reached for her and caught her forearm. He hadn't come here to have her give him the cold shoulder. He came here to talk, and he wouldn't leave until they did. She turned, and Brodie didn't imagine the glare she sent his way. So much for being thankful he'd saved her from a nasty fall.

"I came to see you, Savvy," he said. "I thought we could get some lunch and talk about Dylan's schoolwork."

"I'm not hungry," she retorted, at the same moment that her stomach growled loud enough to rival any of Brodie's athletes' after nine innings.

Her grandmother giggled. "See, dear, obviously you are," she said. "And this display looks just fine as is, so don't worry about adding those other rafting items. Less is more, and all that." Her smile stretched into her cheeks, and she seemed pleased with this turn of events.

Brodie clamped his jaw to keep from grinning at his ally.

Savvy, however, wasn't smiling.

Undeterred, Brodie asked, "So now's a good time for lunch…?"

"Sure it is," Jolaine answered. "And take all the time you need, dear. We're running ahead of schedule." She shoved Savvy gently toward the door. "Y'all enjoy your lunch," she said, and actually chuckled as she continued nudging Savvy out and then yanked the door closed.

"You still like the cheeseburgers at Nelson's?" he asked as though he hadn't noticed her grandmother's not-so-discreet manipulation.

She nodded. What else could she do? If she tried to go back into the store, chances were Jolaine would push—or kick—her back out. Realizing exactly where Savvy got her feistiness, he checked his grin again.

They started walking the short distance to the variety store, merely three doors down from Bowers Sporting Goods, and Brodie took the opportunity to explain why he'd shown up at her workplace in the middle of the day. "I know you don't want to spend any more time with me than necessary, but I believe it's important that we come up with a good game plan for helping the kids, don't you think?"

"Sure," Savvy said, either because she believed it, or because chances were her grandmother wouldn't let her back in the sporting-goods store if she returned too soon, so she had no choice but to talk to Brodie. Either way, he'd take it.

They walked in front of Crowe's Barbershop, and the door beside the red-and-white-striped pole swung open, and Mr. Crowe exited. "Brodie Evans, why, I'll be! It *is* you. I heard you hit the big time when you took that Stockville coaching job. Kind of thought you'd eventually come back around and visit with the old-timers." He pointed toward his shop, where several elderly gentlemen filled the chairs lining each wall. "All of the regulars still come to catch up on the sports in town and drink coffee between cuts and shaves. We'd sure love to have you stop on by."

"I've been pretty busy in Stockville with the team, Mr. Crowe, but I did plan to come back and see you."

"And get a haircut?" the old man prompted.

Brodie grinned. "Yes, sir."

"I'll give your team a discount if they want to get theirs cut here, too. I bet a lot of those young'uns have no idea what's involved in a *real* haircut. Most those newfangled big-city shops don't have a straight razor in the place."

"And no hot towels on the face before the shave and after," Brodie said.

The old man draped an arm around Brodie. "That's my boy. You remember the way it should be done. You come in when you need a cut, and bring your team."

Brodie nodded. "I'll do that."

Mr. Crowe removed his arm from Brodie and beamed at Savvy. "Heard about you taking those children in. That's a good thing, young lady. A real good thing."

Savvy visibly swallowed. "Thank you."

The door to the barbershop opened again, and a man with thinning gray hair, leathery skin and a snarl exited.

"Frank, you see who's back in town?" Mr. Crowe asked.

Brodie didn't recognize the man at first, but as he shook his head disgustedly, the pieces fell into place. Frank Jackson, Willow's father. Brodie hadn't seen him all that often growing up because Willow did her best to stay away from home and her father never showed up at any of her school activities.

"You two, together." Frank growled the words at Brodie and Savvy. "Nothing but trouble, the both of you. Always getting Wendy in trouble back then, too. And you." He pointed to Savvy. "You think you're gonna make something out of those kids? Trouble spews trouble. We tried to tell her, but she'd never listen."

Savvy's eyes narrowed. "They're your grandchildren."

He waved his finger in her face. "They're no part of me, none at all. Because she didn't want to be. Never listened. Went off and got pregnant—twice—and died without ever having a husband. She was a disgrace, that's what she was."

Brodie took a step forward, but Mr. Crowe shuffled between him and Frank.

"Hey, now, Frank, calm down," the barber urged. "You're upset and saying things you don't mean."

"I mean every word," he said through gritted teeth. "These two were the reason she turned her back on her family, the reason she destroyed her life."

"No, sir, we weren't," Brodie said, the calmness of his voice disguising the anger he felt. He'd seen the bruises on Willow and the scars from cigarette burns. This man was the reason she'd left her birth family behind and fought to have what she'd always wanted—a real family of her own.

"You. You're the one who hurt her the most," Frank said, reaching past Mr. Crowe to shove his finger at Brodie's chest.

Again, Brodie remained calm, though he couldn't control his hands clenching into fists, while several of the older men exited the barbershop. "No, sir," he repeated. "I didn't hurt her the most. You did."

"You think I don't know what you did, son?" A thick vein bulged on Frank's forehead.

Brodie wondered if Mr. Jackson knew about what had really happened between him and Willow, but then he pushed that thought away. If Willow had told anyone beyond Savvy, it sure wouldn't have been her father.

"Come on, Frank. There's no need to start anything now," Mr. Crowe coaxed.

Three more men moved toward Willow's father, who was now visibly shaking with rage. Then the group guided Frank away as he spewed hateful words toward Brodie and Savvy. Brodie's entire being burned to hurt the man, but he remained completely still, waiting until the men rounded the corner and were out of sight.

"Thank you for restraining yourself, Brodie. You'd have harmed him if you had reacted," Mr. Crowe said. "I have a soft spot for ol' Frank, but he's got more than a little animosity toward y'all. I had no idea he'd attack you like that or I wouldn't have come out here when I did. But Frank, he's sour on the inside, one of those who ain't happy unless he's making someone miserable, you know?"

"I know." In fact, Brodie knew Frank Jackson

had spent a large portion of his life making his daughter miserable.

After Mr. Crowe returned to his shop, Savvy said, "You've changed a lot."

He inhaled heavily, let the breath out slowly. "I won't argue with you there."

"In high school, you'd have knocked him to the ground and probably kept swinging until someone pulled you off," she said. "But you didn't. You stood there, and you took it, all those hateful things he said. Why?"

Brodie started walking again, and Savvy joined into step. "A month ago I'd have probably knocked him to the ground and kept swinging, but a lot has changed in the past month." He thought about the moment he had gotten that phone call saying that his daughter might not make it through the night. "I've seen how terrible it is to make a mistake and never do anything to rectify it. And I've learned how it feels to realize you'll never have a chance to tell someone you're sorry."

They reached the variety store, and he opened the door for Savvy to enter first, then he followed her to a booth near the front window. "And I think there was more to Mr. Jackson's fury today than his animosity toward us. I think he's madder at himself than anyone else because he knows he didn't do Willow right. And he'll never get the chance to tell her he was wrong."

"Is that how you feel—about Willow and the fact that you never got to tell her you were sorry?" Savvy asked.

"Yes," he said as Marvin Tolleson, the owner of Nelson's Variety Store, arrived at their table.

"Brodie and Savvy, so good to see you two." He handed each of them a laminated menu. "I read about you coaching at the college, Brodie. It's great to have the hometown hero back. And, Savvy, your granddad told me about you taking care of Willow's children. Bless her soul, she sure was dealt a tough row to hoe while she was here, wasn't she?"

"Yes, she was," Savvy agreed. She frowned, and Brodie suspected that she also wondered how often their friend faced her father's rage growing up.

"Well, I'm glad she knew she could count on you to take care of those kids. That right there is what it's all about, I say. Helping others the way God intended." His voice filled with emotion. "Willow had been bringing the kids to church for the past couple of months or so. You'll be bringing them now, I suppose."

Brodie watched as a myriad of emotions played across her face. When she didn't answer, Brodie said, "If Savvy isn't able to bring them, maybe I could."

"We'd love to see all of you there," Marvin said,

still looking at Savvy as though he waited for her to say she'd come.

She didn't.

Brodie wanted to bail her out of the uncomfortable conversation, so he said, "I think we can go ahead and order, Mr. Tolleson."

"We can?" she asked, probably because she hadn't even looked at the menu.

"I think so," he answered, knowing he hadn't looked at his menu, either.

"All righty, what'll you have?" Marvin asked.

"I'll take a double hamburger, hold the tomato and add bacon. She'll want a cheeseburger, with extra pickles and ketchup on the side. And we'll split a large order of sweet potato fries." He glanced at Savvy. "Sweet tea?"

She stared at him.

"Isn't that what you want?" he asked.

"Exactly," she mumbled.

Marvin winked at them. "Gotcha. Mae will bring it out in a jiffy." Then he darted to another table to take dessert orders.

Brodie grinned. "Don't look so surprised. You ordered the exact same thing every time we came here in high school. And if Willow were here, I'd have ordered her a BLT, hold the T, and put—"

"Mayonnaise on the side," she interjected. "And a milk shake, half vanilla and half chocolate."

Brodie's attention moved to her left, and Savvy

tilted her head to also take in the empty end of the booth. Willow's spot.

"Still can't quite grasp it," he said hoarsely.

Savvy didn't have to ask what he meant. "Me, either." She leaned forward and folded her hands together on the table. "And I also can't grasp that she wanted *me* to raise Dylan and the girls. I know her parents weren't an option. But am I that much better?"

He encircled her hands with his, and thankfully, Savvy didn't pull away. "Willow wouldn't have given the kids to you if she didn't think you were the absolute best person to raise them. And you *can* do this, Savvy. I know you can." He squeezed gently. "You're already showing that you're doing a great job."

"How?"

He wiggled his eyebrows. "You've hired a terrific tutor, for starters."

Savvy laughed. "And a modest one. By the way, I don't recall hiring you. Shouldn't we have discussed that? How much do I pay you?"

He shook his head. "This is what Willow wanted. That's payment enough. Besides, my tutoring is a community service. I don't expect or desire to be paid."

Their hands were still entwined in the center of the table, and she slid hers free. Brodie assumed she was battling her emotions, maybe wanting to see him as a friend and an ally to help her through this tough time, but also unwilling to forgive him for turning his back on her and Willow in the past. They'd been close enough, once upon a time, to read each other's thoughts, so Brodie was fairly certain he pegged hers right now.

"Looks like our food is here," he said as Mae Tolleson, a tiny lady with silver hair and a sweet smile, brought their plates to the table.

"Here you go, Savvy." She placed the cheeseburger plate in front of her. "And here's yours, Brodie," she said, giving him the thick, stacked burger. "Your sweet potato fries will be out in a minute. Is there anything else I can get you?"

"I don't think so," Brodie said, then looked to Savvy. "You need anything else?"

"No, Miss Mae. Thank you."

The lady nodded, turned and then stopped. "That was quicker than I thought. Here come your fries now."

A pretty young waitress Brodie didn't recognize brought the oval plate to the table. She had long brunette hair, big blue eyes and a wide smile. She placed the plate of fries between Savvy and Brodie, and then she stood there, gawking...at Brodie.

He smiled, as politely as possible given the extent of her staring, and then turned his attention to his plate.

"Lacy, you can head on back to the kitchen now," Mae said matter-of-factly.

"Oh, right. Yes, ma'am," the girl replied, giggling before leaving.

"You still have a way with the girls, don't you?" Mae tapped Brodie's shoulder. "Lacy brought in that article when you were in the paper. She pinned it up on the bulletin board at the back of the kitchen. I think she's starstruck, even if she's quite a bit younger than you. The price of fame, I suppose?"

Savvy peered after the girl. "How old is she? Nineteen?"

"Twenty-one," Mae said with a laugh. "I'll steer her in the right direction. Bless her heart, always looking for love in all the wrong places." She sighed, then glanced at Savvy. "I used to say that about sweet Willow. So sad she never found it."

Savvy's eyes instantly glistened with tears. "Yes, ma'am."

Mae looked at her sympathetically, sighed again, then turned and went to the kitchen while Brodie reached a hand across the table toward Savvy. "Want me to say grace?"

She looked at his hand. "Seriously?" she asked.

"Seriously."

"O-kay." She slid her hand in his, and he immediately clasped his fingers with hers.

"Dear Father, bless Savvy and everything

that she's doing for the lives of Willow's children. Bless me as I try to help her. And bless this food that we're about to eat. In Your Son's name, amen."

Brodie released her hand and then returned his attention to his plate. "So let's talk about Dylan's schoolwork," he began.

"Wait," she said, while he took a man-size bite of his burger. "I have to say something."

He hummed his contentment with the bite, chewed a bit more, swallowed and then took a big sip of tea. "Okay. Go ahead."

"You *have* changed."

He'd picked up his burger again and taken another bite, but even amid chewing, he couldn't stop his smile.

"Why do you seem so happy?" she asked bluntly.

He swallowed, took another sip of tea and then smiled again. He couldn't help it. "Because for the first time, I'm doing the right thing. And it feels good."

Savvy's eyebrows dipped, mouth slid to the side in confusion. Obviously, she didn't know what to say to that.

"You did want that cheeseburger, didn't you? Because it's gonna get cold if you don't start eating. And if it's still there when I finish, who knows? I might be able to eat it, too," he said.

Savvy all but snarled at him, then she picked up the burger and moaned through the bliss of melted cheddar cheese over a thick beef patty, crisp iceberg lettuce, fresh sliced tomato and those extra pickles captured in the middle of one of Miss Mae's special toasted sourdough buns. "Wow," she said, and promptly took another bite.

Brodie laughed. "A shame we didn't appreciate these things this much when we were in high school. We'd have eaten here every day."

She grabbed a sweet potato fry, took a bite and pointed the rest of it at Brodie. "Definitely. But you do see the problem with this, don't you?" She popped the remainder of the fry in her mouth.

"What's that?"

"I work three doors down. I'll be eating here every day and will probably end up as big as the side of a house. My metabolism isn't what it was back in high school."

"Hey, you didn't weigh anything in high school, and you still don't. And I don't care if you came in here three times a day, you'd still be just right." He watched her slight look of surprise at his compliment, but he wasn't apologizing for stating the truth.

So he continued eating as though he hadn't said anything flattering, and Savvy continued as though she hadn't taken it that way.

"I'm assuming Dylan's teachers identified the

subjects he needs the most help in to pass those standardized tests?" Brodie asked between bites.

"I received a detailed report from his principal. Dylan is doing okay—not great, but okay—in social studies and science. He's failing, though, in prealgebra and reading. Those are the things he'll need to pass on the test next month in order to be promoted."

"Reading?" Brodie asked. "He's having trouble reading?"

"Reading comprehension," Savvy corrected. "The principal said Dylan has no trouble reading the assignments, but he doesn't process the information he reads."

Brodie tossed another sweet potato fry in his mouth and chewed, thoroughly enjoying the combination of salty-sweet perfection. "Algebra wasn't my strong suit, but I can handle helping him out in prealgebra," he said. "And I'm all over that reading comprehension. I had the same problem when I was his age. I know exactly how we'll tackle it."

"You do?" Her surprised tone made him laugh, but he wasn't insulted.

"Yes, I do. In fact, we'll start working on both subjects this afternoon. And I can help him pass that test."

"You sound so confident," she said. "I wish I felt that secure about helping the girls with their reading. Principal Randolph—who ended up being Micca Landry, by the way—said they're struggling with sight words they should've learned in kindergarten."

Brodie stopped eating. "*Micca*? Micca is the elementary school principal?"

"Yes," Savvy said, and grabbed a handful of fries.

Brodie hadn't forgotten what had happened at the senior prom. "How was that? Seeing her again and finding out she's the one who'll make the decision about the girls? You two didn't exactly part high school on good terms."

Savvy dropped the fries on her plate and pushed it to the middle of the table. "I know. I couldn't believe it when I walked in that office and saw her on the other side of the desk."

Even though Brodie had a half dozen fries to be eaten, he pushed his plate forward, too. "So what did you do?"

"I told her I was wrong back then, that I shouldn't have left the prom with her date, and I asked her not to hold her feelings toward me against Rose and Daisy. And then I asked that they be reevaluated in May."

"And?" he prodded.

"And she said she wouldn't let what I did affect her decision about the girls."

Brodie's smile was instant. "That's great, Savvy."

"Yeah," she admitted, "it is. But I still have to get them to pass that test."

He withdrew his wallet and tossed a twenty and a five on the table to cover their lunches and the tip. Then he stood. "I've got an idea about how you can help the girls. Think you can take another fifteen minutes to check it out?"

She paused as if debating whether she wanted to spend any more time with him, but apparently her desire to help the kids won out over her desire to stay away from Brodie. "Sure, fifteen minutes will be fine."

They left the variety store, and he led Savvy toward the other side of the square.

"Where are we going?" she asked, squinting at the row of stores ahead of them.

He stopped in front of A Likely Story, pointed at the surplus of books on display in the window and then opened the door for Savvy to enter.

"The bookstore?" she questioned, but went inside.

Brodie followed her in. "The girls are struggling with reading, and so is Dylan. Surely we can get some things here to help them out. I wonder if Mrs. Presley still runs this place."

A pretty blonde tucked a book into place at the end of one of the aisles and then walked toward them. "Actually, that's my husband's grandmother," she said, grinning. "She left the store to him when she passed on to her reward, and we run it now. I'm Laura, David's wife. He had to go to the post office, but I can help you."

"That'd be great. I'm Brodie Evans, and this is Savvy Bowers. I remember David. He was a little younger than us, but we knew him growing up."

"I'll be sure to tell him you were here," she said, and then she looked at Savvy. "You're James and Jolaine Bowers's granddaughter, right? And Willow's friend?"

"Yes, I am."

"Oh, I'm so glad you came by. I was going to try to get in touch with you today."

"You were?" Savvy asked in surprise.

"Yes," Laura said. "Willow had ordered a few things for Dylan and the girls, and they arrived this week. I heard at church that you were taking care of the children, so I wanted to get the things she ordered to you."

"Thanks for letting me know."

"My pleasure. I'd planned to go to the sporting-goods store after the babies wake up from their nap, but they're taking an extralong one this morning." She pointed toward a small crib near the checkout counter. "Grace and Joy."

"Oh, my, they're beautiful," Savvy said, her hand covering her mouth as she took in the dozing infants. "How old are they?"

"Sixteen months," Laura said. "Willow had

been giving me tips on how she cared for her twins when they were babies. I really liked Willow. I hate it that I didn't get to know her for longer. She was such a sweet person."

"Yes, she was," Savvy said.

Brodie noticed her eyes growing moist, and he didn't want to see her cry again, so he asked, "What did Willow purchase for the kids?"

Laura moved to the other end of the counter. "She got the eighth-grade assigned-reading novel for Dylan, and some Bible storybooks for the girls, along with flash cards." She thumbed through a box filled with books. "Here are Willow's things." She withdrew a bound stack. "Let's see, *The Adventures of Tom Sawyer* for Dylan. That's the novel he needs to read for school. And these beginning-reader storybooks for the girls. She also ordered Bibles. They're in this other box." Laura placed the first stack on the counter, then probed through a second box until she removed the three books: a leather Bible for Dylan and two small children's picture-version Bibles for Rose and Daisy.

"She bought them Bibles," Savvy whispered.

Laura ran her hand across Dylan's name, inscribed in gold at the bottom of his Bible. "They'd only recently started going to church, but it was important to Willow. She said she wanted her kids to know they were loved, not only by her but by

God." She lifted the other two small Bibles and held them so Savvy and Brodie could see Daisy and Rose's names, also inscribed in gold. "She had them engraved. That's why we had to special order them."

"I'm sure it will mean a lot to the children…" Savvy hitched in a breath, apparently at a loss for words.

"We'd grown close," Laura confided, placing the Bibles beside the other items. "Maybe because of the twins, or maybe because of our similar pasts. I want you to know if there's anything we can do to help you, then we want to. David and I both thought a lot of Willow."

Brodie wondered what she meant by "similar pasts," and Laura must have realized she'd left that question unanswered.

"I was pregnant with the girls when I came to Claremont. God brought me to this town, and he brought me to David. David loves me, and he loves the girls." She ran a hand over the top of the Bibles. "I think God put Willow and me in the same place, too. For some reason, she found she could talk to me, and I'm glad for that."

Savvy thumbed through the other stack and stopped when she got to the two boxes of flash cards. "Sight words."

"See there, Willow knew what they needed,"

Brodie said. "She'd have helped them pass those tests, like we're going to do for her now."

"Willow mentioned that the girls were having a tough time with reading," Laura murmured. "Those cards should help. I'd asked her about putting the girls in the book club for kids their age, and Dylan in the one for his age, but she hadn't signed them up yet."

"Book clubs?" Brodie asked. "That might be helpful. Savvy, what do you think?"

"I'm not sure," she said.

"If you want to let them try it, the girls would be in our Monday-afternoon book club. It's for kindergarteners and first graders. For that age, it's mainly a time for them to come in and hear a story. I've been reading The Magic Tree House books to that group. I call it a book club so they'll feel a part of something bigger, something that the older kids and adults do."

"Great idea," Brodie said.

"Thanks. Dylan's group meets on Thursdays, so their meeting is tonight," Laura said. "But when I asked Willow about him joining, she didn't think he'd enjoy it."

"But that might help him with his reading comprehension, if he could discuss what he'd read with other kids," Savvy countered. "What do you think, Brodie?"

He was happy to see she included him in her

decision, especially about Dylan. He might have spent only a little time with the teenager, but he already sensed a kindred spirit. "I'd like to try to help him on my own first," he said, and then explained to Laura, "Willow had contacted me about tutoring Dylan, and we're starting this afternoon."

"The last time I saw her at church, she mentioned trying to find a tutor," Laura told him. "That's wonderful that she'd already found someone and that you're going to start working with him today."

Brodie didn't explain that he'd never actually talked to Willow. But he had come to help Dylan, and Willow's death wouldn't change that. So instead of offering an explanation, he simply said, "Thanks."

"Savvy, one of the books Willow ordered for Dylan hasn't come in yet. If you want to check back with me in a couple of days, it should be here."

"I will." Savvy scooped up the stack of books and flash cards. "What do I owe you?"

"It's already covered." Laura tidied a stack of bookmarks by the cash register.

"Willow paid for them already?" Savvy asked, attempting to grab the stack of Bibles with her other hand.

"I'll get those," Brodie said, picking them up.

"Thanks," Savvy said, then asked again, "Laura, did Willow pay for these already?"

"No, but you're not going to, either. They're a gift, from David and me."

Savvy's forehead creased with her frown. "I can't let you do that."

"Are you really going to take that star from our crown?" Laura asked, smiling.

Brodie hadn't heard that saying in a long time, since he lived in Claremont, but it did ring true. David and Laura wanted to help Savvy, and they weren't going to let her stop them.

When Savvy didn't say anything, Laura added, "We want to, Savvy. There are a lot of people in town who cared about Willow and her children. People like us, who'll only feel better if you allow us to help you out every now and then." One of the babies started squirming in the crib, and Laura scooped her up and cuddled her. "But if you *really* want to do something to pay us back…"

Savvy blinked a couple of times, swallowed thickly. "Yes, I do."

"Then let us see the kids at church with their new Bibles," she said, her smile growing brighter with the idea. "That'd make us happy, and I'm sure it would've made Willow happy, too." Joy whimpered. "I've got to get her fed. Y'all have a blessed day," Laura said, moving away from the checkout counter.

Brodie took that as their cue to go. "You have a blessed day, too," he said, leading Savvy out.

She didn't say a word until they were nearly back to her grandparents' store.

"You know how people are here. When they tell you they want to help you with the kids, they mean it, and it really does make them feel happy to do it." He stepped in front of her and waited until those dark eyes looked up at him.

"She wants me—expects me—to bring them to church. And I can't go back there again."

Brodie stopped at the entrance to Bowers Sporting Goods. "You can't?" Granted, he didn't know what her religious situation had been since she left Claremont, but he wouldn't have imagined she'd turned so far away from God that she wouldn't be willing to take Willow's kids to church.

She glanced at the stack of Bibles in his hand. "You can bring those over when you come to work with Dylan, okay?"

"Sure," he replied. "But do you want to talk about—"

"No," she said, opening the door. "I don't want to talk about it." Then she entered the store, leaving Brodie standing outside, his hand filled with Bibles and his mind filled with questions.

Chapter Seven

"I think I've got dividing fractions okay now," Dylan said.

They'd been sitting at the picnic table for two hours, ever since he got home from school, working on problem after problem in his prealgebra book. The picnic table sat near the edge of the woods, far enough from the trailer to give them a little privacy from Savvy and the girls. She had Rose and Daisy playing on the swing set, and the twins liked to squeal each time Savvy pushed them higher.

"I think you've got it, too," Brodie agreed. He'd realized that part of Dylan's difficulty stemmed from him feeling alone in the endeavor. He'd get started and then frown, frustrated, until Brodie offered the kind of encouragement he needed to motivate him to continue working it out and get the right answer.

"Ready to move on to reading?" Brodie asked.

"Haven't we done enough today?" Dylan scowled. "We didn't spend this much time practicing baseball yesterday."

Brodie laughed. "We actually spent more, but as the saying goes, time flies when you're having fun."

"I'll say. And I'm definitely *not* having fun today." Dylan thumped his pencil against the table.

"Yeah, I get that, but we've got to push through this today, and then we'll move to baseball tomorrow. Passing that test next month is important."

Dylan groaned. "Yeah, I know. I don't wanna be stuck in eighth grade when everyone else moves up to high school."

"Exactly. So let's work on your reading. How about it?"

"If we have to." Dylan huffed out a breath and shrugged his shoulders, which were broad in spite of his lean physique. Brodie suspected when the kid filled out, he'd be a decent size, probably perfect for baseball.

Overlooking the teenager's lack of enthusiasm, Brodie forged ahead. "Did your aunt Savvy bring you the Tom Sawyer book she picked up for you?"

"It's in my room." He glanced toward the trailer. "I need to get it?"

Brodie shook his head. "Not yet." He pulled a folded paper from his pocket. "Let me show you this first." He flattened the sheet and placed it in front of Dylan.

The kid scanned the page. "Hey, this is a test."

Brodie nodded. "On the first five chapters of *The Adventures of Tom Sawyer.*"

Dylan's eyes widened in disbelief. "You're giving me a test before I read it?" He looked at him as if he'd gone crazy. "I have enough trouble passing a test when I *have* read a book. There's no way I'll pass one for something I haven't read." He pushed the paper toward Brodie. "Forget it."

Brodie slid the paper back. "I'm not asking you to *take* the test. I just want you to read the questions."

"Read the questions," Dylan repeated, his tone insinuating Brodie wasn't thinking straight.

"Yes, out loud." Brodie tapped his finger on the first question.

Dylan frowned, but then read, "Number one. How did Aunt Polly find out Tom skipped school to go swimming?" He looked at Brodie, who pointed to the next question.

Dylan huffed another exaggerated breath, but continued. "Number two. When Tom says to the new kid, 'For two cents I will do it,' what does the new kid do?"

"Keep going," Brodie repeated.

"I'm telling you I don't know any of these answers."

When Brodie merely stared at the page, Dylan continued reading the remainder of the questions. After he finished, he picked up the paper and dropped it to the table. "I can't pass this test. I haven't read the chapters. And even after I read the chapters, I won't pass it. That's what I do. I read it, I take the test and I fail. Every single time."

"And *that's* the reason I gave you the test first. So you'll look for the answers as you read the first five chapters. I'll give you two nights to read them, tonight and tomorrow night," Brodie said. "And I do understand. Your ability to read is fine, but you have trouble remembering what you read, right? You have trouble with comprehension."

Dylan nodded. "Yeah, that's it."

"I had the same problem when I was your age," Brodie said. "And I had this amazing teacher, Mrs. Danielson, who learned if I searched for answers as I read, I remembered the story better."

"So she gave you the test first, before you read the book? That doesn't seem fair to the other kids."

Brodie smirked. "She didn't give me *the* test. She gave me *a* test. It might have questions that would be on the actual test, and it might not, but it helped me pay attention to what I read." He tapped the paper. "So I'm going to give you tests as you read Tom Sawyer, and then you'll look for the answers along the way."

"And you think this will help me at school?"

"Definitely." Brodie had learned encouragement went a long way with Dylan. "You'll get used to looking for the answers to questions, and eventually you'll figure out what things might be asked on tests. That'll help you retain those bits of information when you take the standardized test, and you'll pass it with flying colors. So... what do you say?"

"All right, I'll try it," he said at last.

"Great." Brodie thumped him lightly on the back. "So tonight and tomorrow night, read for a while before you go to bed. If you feel like reading three chapters tonight, read three. If not, read two and read the other three tomorrow night. And since my team has an away game this weekend, I won't be here to work with you on Saturday, so I'm going to leave you the test for the next five chapters, too."

"Does that mean we won't practice baseball tomorrow?" Dylan asked glumly.

Brodie shook his head. "I wish we could, but we'll have to wait until Monday. We head out tomorrow for a tournament in Knoxville and won't be back until then. So we'll start with baseball again Monday. Will that work?"

"I guess," Dylan said. "But what about the fractions? Do you think I'm ready for that test? It's tomorrow."

"Let's do a few more to make certain." He looked up to see Savvy had moved away from the girls and held her hand above her eyes to shield the late-afternoon sun as she looked toward Dylan and Brodie. When she saw him, she held up the okay sign and tilted her head, silently asking how he and Dylan were doing. Brodie glanced at Dylan, breezing through the next set of problems in his prealgebra book, and gave her a thumbs-up.

Savvy's responding smile did something strange to his pulse. Or maybe it was the way she looked, with her hair pulled up in a messy ponytail, hardly any makeup, a faded T-shirt, cutoff jeans and flip-flops. Maybe it didn't have anything to do with the way she looked, but with the way she took care of the girls, pushing them on the swing and chatting with them, rubbing a hand along their blond pigtails as she gave them reassuring smiles. She'd be a terrific mom one day. Or rather, she *was* a terrific mom today, to Willow's kids.

He thought of her comment that she couldn't go back to church. Dylan needed church. All of these kids needed church. They needed God, especially now. And so did Savvy. Brodie hadn't realized how much he'd missed God in his life until Marissa's accident, but ever since he'd turned to Him, Brodie felt different, and in a very good way. Savvy had no idea what she was missing.

He planned to show her, somehow.

Dylan placed his pencil on the table, extended his hands over his head and arched his back. "Man, I hate this stuff."

"Prealgebra?" Brodie asked.

One corner of Dylan's lip curved up. "School in general. I just wanna, I don't know, play baseball."

Brodie had said something very similar once upon a time. "I remember the feeling, but an education is important for the rest of your life, so you should keep up the studying, in addition to baseball."

Dylan jerked his head to the right to toss the long hair out of his eyes. Brodie thought about asking if he wanted to visit Mr. Crowe's shop to take care of that nuisance, but he suspected Dylan liked it. The boy did the head jerk with an "I'm cool" air, and Brodie recalled the importance of looking good at that age.

"Did you try it?" Dylan asked. "Playing baseball, like, professionally?"

"I did," Brodie admitted. "Didn't make it all that far, got sent back to the minors after only a brief stint in the majors. But I did okay."

"That helped you get the job you have now, right? Coaching at a college?"

Brodie could see the wheels turning in the kid's mind and wanted to steer him clear of any misconceptions. "Yeah, it helped, but they'd never have hired me if I hadn't gotten my high school diploma and my college degree."

Dylan dropped his head back, looked at the sky and sighed. "Figures."

Again, Brodie laughed. The boy had gotten comfortable around him through yesterday's baseball practice and today's prealgebra. He could sense Dylan relating to him, which was only natural, because they were very similar in their thoughts and dreams, or at least the thoughts and dreams Brodie remembered having as a teenager. He enjoyed talking with Dylan, and Dylan seemed to enjoy talking with Brodie, as well. Even so, he wasn't prepared for Dylan's next question.

"Do you think if I'd gotten help quicker, she'd have lived?" he asked quietly, still looking at the cobalt sky. His Adam's apple bobbed after the question, and Brodie knew that, in spite of being able to joke around with Brodie throughout the afternoon, Dylan was still hurting. And missing his mom.

Give me the right words, Lord.

"No, Dylan. If God was ready for your mom to be in heaven, then she was going there."

Dylan took his attention from the sky to Brodie. His eyes glistened, but he held the tears at bay.

"She was gonna tell me about my dad that day."

Dylan's pain-filled statement punched Brodie as if he'd been hit in the chest by a line drive. Again, he prayed for words, but this time none came. Because Dylan needed to say more.

"I turned thirteen three weeks ago, and Mom said we'd celebrate by camping and hiking for spring break—just the two of us—and that she had something to tell me when we were there. She wanted to tell me at Jasper Falls. Rose and Daisy stayed with Miss Mandy while we went. So it was just us."

There was a long pause. Dylan pulled his hands to the edge of the picnic table and gripped it, as if he needed to hold on to something before continuing. "I'd been asking her about my dad for forever, and I just knew she was going to tell me that day." He blinked, swallowed. "We hiked up to the halfway part, you know, where that big rock is."

"I know where it is," Brodie said. He, Willow and Savvy had often hiked to the massive rock, where he'd jump or dive into the water, and the girls had usually tanned in the sun.

"She wanted to stop there, sit down and talk. That's what she said—that she wanted to talk there." He returned his gaze to the sky and blinked several times, still visibly struggling to contain his emotions.

"She slipped from the rock?" Brodie asked, unable to see that happening. That midpoint wasn't all that far above the falls. Willow had jumped from there several times when they were teenagers. She and Savvy would sunbathe until they got hot and then jump in to cool off. Brodie didn't see how a fall from that point would have caused her death.

Dylan sat silent for a moment, then slowly shook his head. "No. That's where she wanted to stop, but I had always wanted to hike to the top…" He took a deep breath, held it a moment, then pushed it out. "I talked her into going up. I knew she was going to tell me about my dad, and I wanted to be somewhere really special when I heard about him. I'd been halfway up before, but I'd never been to the top, and I really wanted to go."

Brodie had hiked to the top of Jasper Falls before, but always with Willow and Savvy watching. They were too scared of the slippery, moss-covered outcroppings along the way, as well as the points where you had to rely on faith to reach out and grab the next protruding rock. The thought of Willow and Dylan trying to make that climb sent a chill to his bones, because he could easily see how she could have slipped, and that fall would have been deadly.

Had been deadly.

"If I hadn't asked her to go up there, she'd still be alive," Dylan said, and he looked at Brodie once more, this time heavy tears streaming from his bright blue eyes. "And I'd know about my dad. But now I never will. And even worse, we've lost our mom. Because of me."

If Brodie knew anything about the boy's dad, he could offer insight, but he was clueless. However, he knew that Willow would never want her son blaming himself for the accident that took her life. "Dylan," he started, but the boy interrupted.

"She named me after my uncle, because he was, like, all great and everything. He was in the army, and he died saving people in Iraq." He paused. "He died a hero, and she wanted me to be like him, but I couldn't save her." He sucked in a big gasp of air, then shook his head again, as if still trying to comprehend what had happened, and why.

If Brodie had all of the answers, he'd give them, but he could only offer the truth. "Dylan, like I said, God was ready for her now, and what happened wasn't your fault. I have no doubt she'd tell you that, if she could. It was an accident."

"That's what everyone keeps saying." He stared

into the woods that led to the mountain. "I'm going for a walk."

Brodie was afraid he'd failed at his attempt to console. *Help me out here, Lord.*

Dylan cleared his throat, pushed up from the table.

"You want to take your Tom Sawyer book along? Maybe get in some of your reading for the night while you're out there?" Brodie asked, grasping at straws for something that would get the teenager to stop thinking about the accident and blaming himself for his mother's death.

Dylan shook his head, the long hair falling forward to shield his eyes. This time he didn't sling it away, and Brodie suspected he was trying to hide his tears.

His heart hurt for the kid, but he didn't know what else to do.

"Will you put these in the house?" Dylan asked, motioning toward the books on the table without looking up. "The trailer," he corrected. "Mom always wanted a house. She asked me about helping her fix this place up, but I never did. I never did a lot of things she wanted me to do."

Brodie knew what that was like, to look at the past and think of all the would'ves and should'ves of missed opportunities. He'd been doing that nonstop over the past two weeks, since he'd learned of Marissa's accident and realized he'd missed so many years with his little girl. But Brodie still had a chance to correct that mistake, because Marissa had survived the accident. Dylan's thoughts of lost opportunities offered no chance for resolution, because his mother was gone.

"I can take 'em," Dylan said, apparently seeing Brodie's silence as a no. He reached for the books.

"I'll get them," Brodie replied, and then God answered his prayer by letting him know exactly what to say to the brokenhearted teenager. "Hey, Dylan, wait a minute. I've got something else that you can take with you while you walk. Something your mother got for you."

"What is it?" Dylan asked, kicking at a clump of dirt on the ground.

Brodie went to his truck and retrieved the Bibles. "She ordered these for y'all before—" he didn't want to say before she died "—your camping trip." Brodie held the brown leather Bible out so that Dylan could see his name on the cover.

Dylan reached for the Bible, took it and then ran a finger across his name. A thick teardrop fell to land above the gold engraving, and he wiped it away.

"You want to take it with you while you walk?" Brodie asked quietly.

Dylan nodded, then turned and made his way to the nearest path within the trees, the Bible clutched in his right hand.

Brodie wasn't surprised when Savvy left the girls playing to come see what had happened with Dylan.

"Is he okay? Where's he going?" she asked, her features etched with concern.

"He's going for a walk," Brodie said. "And he took his Bible. I'm guessing he needs to think, maybe time to pray or read his Bible."

"Do you think— Should I try to find a therapist for him? Like a grief counselor? He's so torn up and seems so broken," she said. "It's hard to know what I should do." Her voice quivered, and Brodie turned to see her quickly flick tears from each cheek. "I…I don't want the girls to see me crying," she whispered.

Brodie glanced toward the back of the trailer. "They're busy taking turns on the slide," he said. "And they aren't looking this way."

"I'm glad for that." She swiped her hands across her face again. "I don't want to make things worse for them. They've been through so much already."

"Savvy, you're not making anything worse. You're making it better. And you're doing exactly what Willow would've wanted you to do— taking care of them all."

"The girls seem like they're doing okay. They miss their mama, but they have each other. They're always together. But Dylan…" She closed her eyes, opened them and peered toward the path he'd taken. "He seems okay one minute and then totally withdrawn the next. I don't know how to help him."

Brodie thought of how quickly Dylan had changed the subject from baseball to his mother's death and understood what Savvy was saying. She deserved to know the truth about why the boy was so troubled. "He's blaming himself for the accident," he said.

"He told you that?" She sounded stunned. "He hasn't said anything to me about it. I keep waiting for him to talk about what happened that day, but he hasn't."

"They were climbing to the top of the falls," Brodie said.

Savvy gasped. "Why? Willow would never go up there. She was more afraid of it than I was."

"Dylan wanted to go," he explained.

"Oh, my," Savvy whispered. "Oh, bless his heart. And he saw her fall. That had to be..." She shuddered. "Brodie, that had to be terrible. And now he blames himself. What did you say when he told you?"

"I told him that God was obviously ready to take her and that it wasn't his fault."

"And how did he respond?"

"He didn't say anything, but he took his Bible along for that walk. I think he just needs time." Brodie remembered what else had been troubling

Dylan and decided to fill Savvy in on that, as well. "He's also having a hard time because he believed she was going to tell him who his father was that day. And now he thinks he'll never know."

Her mouth dropped open; then she covered it with her hand.

"Do you know who Dylan's father is?" Brodie would've thought that if Willow had told anyone, it would have been Savvy.

But she shook her head. "No, I don't. Willow only said that he wasn't in the picture and that she didn't want to talk about him. And since I hadn't been around any during that time, I don't even know who she was dating." She looked toward the girls, still playing, then lowered her voice. "It's awful to say this now, but I always suspected Willow might not know who Dylan's daddy was, so I didn't ask a lot of questions because I didn't want to make her feel bad."

"You were just trying to give her what you thought she needed at the time."

She stood silent for a moment. "But maybe I *should* have asked. Then I'd know, for Dylan." She swiped at her wet cheeks again. "I feel like such a lousy friend."

Brodie didn't think before reacting. She was upset, and he couldn't merely stand here and watch her cry. He wrapped an arm around her and gently drew her against his chest.

She didn't stop him. On the contrary, she clenched her fingers into his shirt and held on. "Brodie, I should've called her more back then. I shouldn't have left her, abandoned her, as a friend. I was only concerned about what was going on in my life, and I didn't even care about what was going on in hers."

"It's okay, Savvy. You're doing fine with the kids. And you were a great friend to Willow." He rubbed a hand up and down her back, offering what little comfort he could. "That's why she entrusted you with her children." He held her close and continued to pray for the right thing to do, the right thing to say.

After a moment of letting him hold her, Savvy nodded against his chest and sniffed. Then she slowly looked up at him. "Thank you," she whispered.

He cradled her face, ran his thumbs along her cheeks to smooth the tearstains away. She was so beautiful, so incredibly compassionate and caring. So concerned for Dylan and the twins. And Brodie found himself lost in the dark chocolate depths of those eyes. He'd promised God he'd get his life right. He'd promised to fix old wrongs and to focus on his job at the college, to turn away from his previous compulsions. But right now he wanted to kiss Savvy. Very much. And this wasn't just any female; this was Savvy. His friend.

He stared at her heart-shaped lips, saw her eyes drift closed and knew that she anticipated the kiss as much as he wanted to give it.

Then the past invaded the present. The last time he'd kissed a friend, they hadn't stopped with a kiss. They hadn't stopped at all.

And he'd lost Willow's friendship...and Savvy's.

Brodie took his hands from her face, cleared his throat and watched her eyes open in surprise.

Then his phone rang in his pocket.

Brodie's heart sputtered in his chest with the sharp sound of reality. He'd nearly kissed Savvy. Nearly fallen down the same path of temptation that had caused him so much trouble before. He shoved his hand in his pocket and withdrew the phone, glanced at Cherie's number on the display.

"I've got to take this," he said gruffly, then answered, "Hello?"

"Um, hi," the voice said on the other end.

"Marissa," he breathed, his eyes locked on Savvy's. "It's—it's my daughter," he told her, and then watched as Savvy's face made a rapid transformation from surprise...to complete and utter shock.

Chapter Eight

It's my daughter.

Savvy barely heard Laura reading the story to Rose, Daisy and the other youngsters during Monday's book club meeting, because she kept hearing Brodie's words, the same way she'd heard them repeatedly in her thoughts all weekend.

If she had it to do over again, she'd have stayed beside him when he took the call and asked him about his little girl. And her mother. He had a daughter. Did he have a wife, too?

And the bigger question: Why should she be bothered if he did? It wasn't as if she was interested in him or anything.

But he'd wanted to kiss her; she was certain of it. And she'd wanted him to; she was also certain of that.

She'd been mad at herself for the past four days over that truth. She had wanted Brodie to kiss her. And wouldn't that have been stupid? For one reason, because he'd hurt Willow in the past, so whether he'd changed or not, he definitely had the capability to inflict pain. And Savvy had been hurt enough. Plus, kissing Brodie would be foolish. And she'd been foolish enough, too, especially when it came to guys who were not available.

And then there was the truth that Brodie would never suspect. Because of the man who'd broken Savvy's heart and stolen her faith, she hadn't wanted to trust again, hadn't wanted to give in to temptation again.

Savvy hadn't kissed anyone…in over ten years.

"Aunt Savvy?" Rose whispered, snapping Savvy back to reality and to the little girl who'd left the reading circle and now stood in front of Savvy.

Savvy noticed something different about Rose today, but she couldn't put her finger on what. She ran a hand along the child's pigtail, smiled at the way the soft blond hair curled around her finger. "What is it, sweetie?"

Rose pressed her small palm against Savvy's cheek. "I love you."

Savvy blinked, swallowed and felt her skin tingle in response to those three precious words. "Oh, Rose, I love you, too."

The little girl smiled, patted Savvy's cheek, then turned to listen to the rest of the story.

Savvy held her close, kissed the top of her head and inhaled the sweet scent of her shampoo. Savvy prayed that somehow Willow knew how much she already cared for her children, and how much she wanted to be a good mother figure to each of them. She felt that she was doing okay with Rose and Daisy. But Dylan… She wasn't sure about Dylan. He'd started to come out of his shell around Brodie, but he and Savvy didn't have that kind of connection, not yet.

What would happen when Brodie stopped coming around to tutor? Or to help with baseball? What would Savvy do to help Dylan when Brodie decided to spend more time with his own child, the daughter who had called Thursday night? Or with the wife sitting at home somewhere, a woman who might or might not have known that he nearly kissed Savvy?

"Aunt Savvy?" Rose asked.

Once again, she jerked her attention away from wandering thoughts of Brodie Evans. "Yes?"

"The story is over," Rose said, and then Savvy realized what was different about the little girl today.

"Rose! You are making your *s*'s! Let me see those new teeth," she said.

Rose gave her the biggest smile she could manage, wide enough to show tiny white teeth and gums, and sure enough, the two top teeth had made a rapid appearance. They weren't all the way out yet, but obviously enough to give her more control of those tough consonants.

"Say my name," Savvy said.

Rose giggled. "Aunt Savvy!"

She scooped the child up and hugged her again. "That's awesome, Rose!"

Still giggling, Rose asked, "Can I go read to the dolls, too, now, like Daisy?"

Daisy had picked up a book and pretended to read to a small group of American Girl dolls near the reading nook. "Sure. Have fun."

Laura watched the interaction and then took the seat beside Savvy. "They're adorable," she said.

"I know," Savvy said.

"I looked for y'all at church yesterday," Laura said softly.

Savvy had thought about it when they woke up Sunday morning, but then she remembered the last time she'd been at the church, how that visit had changed her life forever, and she'd kept the kids at home. "We didn't make it," she answered.

Laura nodded, as though that explanation was enough, which was good, because that was all Savvy was willing to give. "I'd better go help David out," Laura said. "He's good at running the cash register, but not when he's holding both of the girls." She laughed, then stood and gave Savvy a smile. "In case no one has told you, I wanted to let you know that you *are* doing a great job with the kids."

"Thanks," Savvy said. In fact, her grandparents had told her as much an hour ago, when she'd left Dylan with them at the store, and Brodie had told her the same thing. Somehow it meant more coming from him. But Savvy wouldn't analyze why.

Daisy noticed Savvy watching them and grinned. "We did it, Aunt Savvy. We read a book all by ourselves!"

Savvy nodded. "I'm so proud of you."

Daisy placed the book back on the shelf. "Can we get ice cream to celebrate?"

"Yes," Rose chimed in. "Can we, Aunt Savvy? Please?" She purposely stretched the *s* out in please.

Savvy laughed. "Sure, we can get ice cream to celebrate. Let's get Dylan first so he can join us."

They left the bookstore and walked along the sidewalk with several people smiling at them along the way. Maybe the town had started forgiving her after all. Or maybe they'd forgotten what she'd been like as a teenager.

Then they passed the front of Scraps and Crafts, and a gray-haired woman exited, her arms holding several colorful skeins of yarn. Savvy recognized Lorina Jackson at once. Willow's mother hadn't aged well, her face drawn and leathery, and her mouth turned down in a permanent frown. She stopped beside them, her attention laser focused on Savvy, and then on each of the girls.

"Come on, Aunt Savvy. Let's get our ice cream!" Rose said, pulling on Savvy's arm when she saw Savvy had slowed her pace.

Savvy had only seen Lorina sporadically throughout their school years, and she hadn't seen her at all after Willow's older brother died. Though Willow hadn't had great parents before his death, after he died, they'd been terrible. Acted as if she didn't exist. Or worse, as if she should bear the brunt of the anger they experienced over his death. Savvy had seen Willow's bruises. She knew what Willow's father had done. And she knew this woman did nothing to stop him.

Should Savvy speak to her now? Acknowledge that this was the girls' grandmother?

Rose and Daisy didn't even recognize the lady.

"Yes," Savvy said. "Let's go get the ice cream." Then she continued walking without looking back. If Lorina wanted to speak to her grandchildren, she'd had an excellent opportunity. Obviously, she didn't. That told Savvy everything she needed to know.

"Hey, there's Dylan," Rose said. "And Mr. Brodie!"

Those last three words caused Savvy to trip on

the sidewalk. She'd like to have blamed a crack, or a rock, a tree root—anything—but there were no obstructions in her path. She simply wasn't prepared to see him yet and her feet knew it. Or maybe she wasn't prepared to see him standing there in that baseball uniform, as handsome as he had been in high school, or maybe even more. More mature, more masculine. And standing there, smiling, beside Dylan, who was also smiling, he looked like…a really good guy.

But was he?

"It's right foot, left foot," he said drolly when they reached the sporting-goods store.

"Very funny," she said.

"We're going to get ice cream to celebrate," Rose said. "Y'all wanna come?"

"What are you celebrating?" Brodie asked with a grin.

"They read a book," Savvy answered.

"All by ourselves!" Daisy added proudly, pigtails bobbing with her excessive nod.

"Now, that is a reason to celebrate," Brodie said to the girls, but then he looked up at Savvy. "Good job, Sav," he quietly added.

"Thanks."

"That's good, Rose and Daisy," Dylan said, but then he said to Savvy, "But I don't need ice cream. We were coming to the bookstore to tell you we're going to the field so I can practice with my new things."

Savvy had been so wrapped up in seeing Brodie that she hadn't noticed the new bat and glove in Dylan's hands. "Did my grandparents give you those?" she asked, but she knew before Dylan answered who had purchased the top-of-the-line bat and glove that Dylan clutched like prized trophies.

"They helped us pick them out," Brodie said.

"Coach Brodie bought them," Dylan clarified, stuffing his hand in the glove and then holding it up as he squeezed in on the fingers. "Look how the leather already moves. That means it's a good glove."

Savvy nodded. "I know. That *is* a good glove." She started to add "But" and then explain why she couldn't let Brodie buy him such an extravagant gift; however, Brodie must have seen where her sentence was heading, because he cut her off before she got the chance.

"Hey, Dylan, why don't you walk the girls to the Sweet Stop while I talk to your aunt Savvy for a second?" he said casually.

"But I'm ready to go to the field," Dylan protested.

"I know... We will. I just need to talk to her first, okay?" He fished a ten out of his wallet and handed it to Dylan. "Here's some money for the ice cream."

"I was going to pay for the ice cream," Savvy countered.

"Go on, and we'll catch up with you there," Brodie continued, as though she hadn't spoken.

Dylan shrugged but steered the girls, chattering about what flavors they wanted, down the sidewalk.

Savvy waited until they entered the sweets store before complaining, "You shouldn't have bought him that bat and glove. Those were the most expensive ones we had in the store, and besides, I had planned to buy him what he needed. I was just waiting to see which kind he preferred."

"So I saved you the trouble of shopping," he said. "He needs to practice with a bat and glove that he'll be using, and I wanted to get him what he needs. It isn't a big deal."

"I know how much those cost," she retorted, "and it *is* a big deal."

"Your grandmother gave me a family discount."

"Family discount?"

He tilted his head toward the store. "I know I'm not family, but I got the impression she didn't want me to argue and wouldn't have listened if I tried."

Savvy started to say he was wrong, but she knew he wasn't. "Even so, I'm going to pay you back."

He shook his head. "Nope, I can't let you."

"Why not?"

"Because I won't let you take that star from my crown." His sly smile said he was proud of scooping up that tidbit from Laura, and Savvy didn't like it. Not one bit.

"That's not fair," she said.

"I'd agree, but I know you can't argue with it, so that's my reasoning."

Dylan stuck his head out of the ice cream shop and yelled, "Y'all want anything?"

"Do you?" Brodie asked Savvy.

Still flustered, she shook her head. "No."

Brodie yelled back, "No, thanks, but get yourself one!"

Dylan nodded and ducked back into the candy store.

Brodie still held his wallet in his hand from getting the money for ice cream, and he slid it in the back pocket of his baseball pants. The uniform made him look more like a player than a coach. And she noticed how he was still in great shape, the muscles of his back evident when he called out to Dylan, and when he turned her way, his shoulders and chest appeared beautifully firm and broad, perfect for holding someone close, making her feel protected. The way he had made her feel when he held her the other night.

Savvy did not like where her thoughts were

headed, and she blamed him for wearing that striking outfit. "In football, basketball, soccer, every other sport, the coach wears regular clothes. Only in baseball does the coach wear a uniform like the players. Why is that?" she blurted.

He laughed. "You really want to know? It's a history lesson, but I have the answer."

"Yes, I do." She'd always been curious, but not for the reasons she asked now. Right now she wanted to know why he had to dress so…appealingly. Maybe not to every female, but definitely to Savvy.

Brodie had no idea why she suddenly had an interest in baseball history, but that was one subject he knew distinctly, so he explained, "Okay, back in the early years of baseball, the person who made decisions during the game was called the captain. He did what the coach does today, but he also played. So the captain wore a uniform because he was also a participant." He cleared his throat. "The tradition continued after captains were called coaches and made decisions from the dugout. Some people say we still wear them because we regularly walk onto the field during the game, either during pitching changes or for other reasons." He grinned. "Say, an argument with an umpire, for example."

Savvy opened her mouth as if she was going

to say something, or ask another baseball trivia question, and Brodie was ready, but then she frowned and shook her head.

"What?" he asked.

"I didn't think we'd see you today," she said.

Brodie had no doubt that wasn't what she'd originally planned to say. In high school, she never held back on her thoughts, not to him or Willow. But a lot had changed since then, and he didn't call her on it. Instead he said, "I thought y'all knew I was planning to take Dylan to the field today. I showed up at the trailer, but you were gone, so I came to your grandparents' store to see if you were there."

She shrugged. "We waited awhile, but I had signed the girls up for the book club, and I couldn't wait any longer." Then she turned toward the hiking display in the store's front window and her eyes widened.

Brodie looked to see what caused the reaction and caught a glimpse of her grandmother, not so discreetly spying on them from behind a rack of baseball jerseys. He grinned, but attempted to act as if he hadn't seen her. "The college set up a charity game this afternoon that I hadn't known about."

"Did you see your daughter this weekend?" she asked, and then bit down on her lower lip as though she could make herself stop talking.

"No, I would've loved that," he said honestly, "but we don't have that kind of relationship, not yet." Brodie didn't want her wondering about his relationship with Marissa, or Cherie. "I should've explained about her, and that phone call, when it happened," he said. "And I would have, if you'd stuck around instead of heading into the trailer without saying goodbye."

Savvy stuffed her hands in the pockets of her shorts. "You don't owe me any explanation. I was just making conversation, wondering if you saw her this weekend." She did a pitiful job of looking as though she didn't care what he'd say next.

"Sure you were." He stepped closer. "And you weren't ticked at the fact that you didn't know I had a daughter, or wondering if I had a wife to go with that daughter? You weren't thinking I was a total jerk because I had someone waiting at home when I nearly kissed you?"

"I was just wondering if you saw her," she repeated, her voice a breathy whisper and her cheeks tinged pink.

He smirked. "Okay, I'll play along. No, I didn't see Marissa this weekend. In fact, I saw her for the first time since she was a baby two weeks ago, when she was in a car accident, and my *ex*-wife called to ask me to come to the hospital." The memory of that rush of emotions when he got her call pierced his heart again. He reminded himself that Marissa had made it through the night. "During that drive to Knoxville, I thought I might never get to see my daughter again. And that phone call was the first time Marissa has ever called me, so it was rather important."

Savvy's eyebrows dipped, her dark eyes studying him as though trying to obtain all of the information she wanted to know from reading his face. But there was too much to tell, and no way she could figure it all out with a glance. "Why hadn't you talked to her?"

Dylan poked his head out of the ice cream shop once, apparently awaiting their arrival. Brodie held up a finger to indicate they were on their way. "I want to talk to you about that, but it'd take longer than the time we have. With your permission, I'd like to come to the trailer an hour before the kids get home tomorrow. We can talk…about things," he said.

"I'll need to check with my grandparents." She pointed toward their store. "But it should be okay."

He grinned. "Your grandmother said it'd be fine."

She shot another look inside the store. "You're sneaky."

"Are you talking about me or her?" he asked, tilting his thumb toward the display window, where he figured Savvy's grandmother hid…somewhere.

She laughed. "Both."

"Maybe so," he agreed, then motioned toward the Sweet Stop. "We should probably go. Dylan's getting anxious." Then he waved toward the woman he finally spotted peeking around a display.

Jolaine waved back.

"Sneaky," Savvy repeated, but also waved to her grandmother.

Brodie grinned. "Persistent, too."

They walked toward the Sweet Stop. "Hey, if she said anything today that made you uncomfortable, I want to apologize."

"She didn't…" he replied, letting the word hang and knowing he needed to say something about the way they'd ended things the other night.

Savvy stopped a few feet before the entrance of the ice cream shop. "What?" she asked.

He took a deep breath then let it out. He needed to choose his words wisely.

As impatient as she'd always been, she asked again. "What is it? Just tell me."

"Okay. We're going to be seeing a lot of each other, with me helping with Dylan, so I don't want anything awkward between us." Rubbing a hand over his jaw, he looked down at her. "Look, I'm trying to do things the right way now, and what I did—*nearly did*—the other night, wasn't right. And I want to apologize."

"Apologize?" she asked.

"Yes," he said. "I started to kiss you. I know it, and you know it. And that was a mistake. I want to let you know that I'm sorry…and it won't happen again."

Chapter Nine

Savvy busied herself in the trailer straightening the kids' rooms, paying bills, doing dishes, anything to pass time while she waited for Brodie. And after she'd cleaned everything that could be cleaned, she still had ten minutes before he was due to arrive. She scanned the trailer, couldn't find a single thing left to do and decided to wait for him on the deck.

Sitting on the wooden steps, she thought about what she should say first. Should she ask him about his daughter? That'd be the smartest subject to start with, she decided as she heard his truck coming up the driveway. Within a minute, it came into view, and she easily saw him, a half smile playing on his lips as he pulled up. The windows were down, and his arm, all muscled and tan, rested on the edge of the driver's-side door.

Last week, she hadn't even looked at him as

he'd neared the trailer. This week, she stared. Because the image of Brodie, pulling up in that black F-150, could easily qualify for a decent ad for Ford. Or a poster of a really good-looking man in a big black truck.

He parked and climbed out, and she took in the difference in his appearance. Today, he wore a sky blue T-shirt, well-worn jeans and hiking boots. She'd been wrong. It wasn't the baseball uniform that was so appealing. It was the man in it. And he was just as attractive today in regular clothes. Or more.

She'd planned to ask him about his daughter. *That* was the most neutral topic of the ones he'd referenced yesterday. But when she opened her mouth, her words wouldn't cooperate.

"Why *didn't* you kiss me?"

Brodie had intended to tell her about his past and why he was so determined to do the right thing now, explain how he wanted them to get along, work together on their goal of helping Willow's kids, and in doing so, prove that he was the kind of man who deserved a place in his daughter's life. In other words, he wanted to be Savvy's friend, the way he was in high school, and he didn't want to mess that up by taking their relationship somewhere it shouldn't go.

But his attention was first diverted by the sight

of her, sitting on the top step of the deck wearing a navy-and-red Braves T-shirt, ragged blue jeans with a rip over the right knee and red sandals. Her hair was pulled up in a high ponytail, but because of the short length, only a little remained captured, the majority of the strands falling loosely around her face. Light red gloss made her lips shine in the sun, and her eyes were, as always, as dark as chocolate.

Surrounding her, several index cards were taped to various parts of the trailer. *Door. Deck. Window. Step. Flowerpot. Red bag.*

The index cards caught his attention, too, but not as much as the pretty lady with her messy hair, tattered jeans and shiny lips.

However, it wasn't her appearance or the index cards that threw Brodie's world off balance; it was her question: *Why* didn't *you kiss me?*

Unfortunately, he'd already started walking toward the deck, so his progression continued, and the old Brodie wanted to answer, "I have no idea, but I'll make up for that now." Then he'd kiss her, and then one thing would lead to another, and…

He reined in that desire. He'd changed. But the fact that Savvy looked at him as though she might be bothered he hadn't kissed her wasn't making this any easier.

"I…" he began, taking a seat on the step beneath hers and focusing on the words he *should* say. "I didn't want to mess up what we have going now, taking care of the kids together, by doing something that wouldn't be smart. I'm trying to do the right thing."

"You're trying to do the right thing?" she repeated.

Brodie nodded but didn't miss the fact that she sounded disappointed. He was disappointed, too. But that didn't change his mind. Kissing Savvy would be a mistake, and he'd made that kind of mistake before. He wouldn't do it again, especially not with someone he cared about as much as he cared about Savvy. And he did care about her. And Dylan. And Rose and Daisy. And Marissa.

He had to remember all of them to control the impulse to do something he might regret. Something that would cost him another friendship.

Brodie prayed he handled this conversation right. And then he said, "Just so you know, I didn't stop because I didn't want to kiss you."

Her eyebrows rose, and she gave him that "So…?" stare that he believed women perfected in the mirror. He'd sure seen it plenty.

He laughed, which probably wasn't the best move, because then she did that folding-her-arms thing coupled with the eyebrow raise.

Brodie held up his hands. "That didn't come out right," he said, and asked God to help him keep his foot out of his mouth. "For you to understand, you've got to know what has happened to me since high school. A lot went on when I played ball in college, during the time when you and I lost contact after you moved to Florida, and the years that came after."

Her pretty dark eyes searched his face, urging him to continue, but she didn't say a word.

He exhaled slowly. "Like I said yesterday, when Marissa called me Thursday night, that was the first time she'd ever called me. We haven't had a relationship, ever, and that's my fault…" Suddenly, his voice trailed off.

"Go on," she said softly. "Please don't stop now."

He raked a hand through his hair, grappling to find the right words to explain how everything had gone terribly wrong. "It's all because of what happened between Cherie and me. We got married because I loved her, and she loved me, but I figured out pretty quickly that I wasn't ready for the kind of commitment Cherie wanted and needed."

"Wait—back up. How did you two get together in the first place?"

"We met that first year I went to UT when we were both freshman. I played baseball. She cheered for football. We hit it off and were crazy about each other." There was a long pause. "At the time, we both thought getting married would be great, but we hadn't dated that long, less than six months, when we headed to Vegas."

"Vegas?" Savvy asked.

"In one of the Elvis chapels. By Elvis," he said. "And no, we weren't drinking. It just sounded like a lot of fun. And we knew we wanted to be together, but the truth was that as much as I loved Cherie and the idea of running off to Vegas and coming back with a wife, I wasn't ready to be a husband." He pressed his lips into a grim line. "Cherie was ready to be a wife. She was all in. But I never gave her what she wanted—a guy who'd be happy, satisfied to stay home with her instead of spending time at the field or going out with the guys. I still wanted to have a good time. A lot.

"And when she got pregnant in that first year of our marriage, she was thrilled. She thought I'd settle down once we had a baby. But I panicked. I wasn't ready to be a father any more than I was ready to be a husband."

"So you asked for a divorce," Savvy said, disappointment evident in the statement.

Brodie deserved that disappointment. The divorce had been his fault, even if he hadn't asked for it or wanted it at the time. "No. I was determined to stay married, even though I wasn't giving a hundred percent. I *never* asked for a divorce, but after Cherie had Marissa, she couldn't take my lack of commitment anymore." Brodie swallowed through the pain of the bitter memory.

"And you didn't even see your daughter?" Savvy asked. "Didn't y'all have joint custody, or something like that? Where you saw her on the weekends, or every other weekend?"

She'd zeroed in on the fact that bothered Brodie the most. But he'd started telling her the truth, and he wouldn't stop now. "I had the right to have Marissa every other weekend. And I took her for a few weekends," he said. "But I didn't know anything about taking care of a baby. She had colic, and she cried unless you held her. She didn't seem to like me either, and would only settle down when I gave her back to Cherie. And most of the weekends, I had baseball practice. Or games."

"So you never saw her?" She gave him a long, level look. "Brodie, I know what that's like, to have a parent you never see because they just don't care enough to see you. My mom wanted her drugs more than she wanted me. I learned to understand that as I got older, but it never made not having a mom any easier. You picked your game over your wife and daughter." Disillusionment filled her words. "That's…so sad."

Brodie had known admitting the truth to Savvy would be hard, but he hadn't thought about the comparison of her own past to his. "I'm not proud of it," he admitted roughly. "I wasn't a father to

Marissa, but she did have a father. A couple of years after we divorced, Cherie met Ryan. He treated her the way she'd always wanted me to treat her. And they were married."

Brodie cleared his throat and asked God to give him the strength to tell Savvy the rest. "After they'd been married awhile, they called me and told me that Marissa had started calling him Daddy, and that they wanted me to terminate parental rights, allow Ryan to adopt Marissa."

"So he became her daddy," Savvy said. "And you've had no place in her life until they called you to the hospital after her accident." Her words were softly spoken, and Brodie got the impression she wasn't judging him. On the contrary, he suspected she felt sorry for him because he'd missed all of those pivotal years. Then she cemented that suspicion with her next words. "I'm sorry that you gave that up, the chance to see her grow. And I can see why that phone call would've meant so much to you."

He wanted to tell her everything, even though this part stung the most. "It did mean a lot to me, because she called. But it wasn't because she really wanted to talk to me. I'd called Cherie that morning to check on Marissa, see how she was healing, and I asked her to tell Marissa I called. She did, and then Marissa called out of the blue." He took a breath, let it out. "To ask me not to call her mom anymore. She thanked me for coming to the hospital but reminded me that I left her and her mom a long time ago."

"Oh, Brodie, I'm sorry..." Savvy murmured.

He nodded. "I'm sorry, too," he said. "And I told her that, and that I hoped that eventually she can forgive me, that she'll actually call me sometime because she does want to talk to me." He thought about how hard it'd been to listen to that line go dead when she ended the call.

"Maybe she'll come around," she said. "She knows that you came to the hospital when you were called. That surely means something to her."

He was glad Savvy didn't merely judge him, that she realized that the mistakes of his past tore him apart now. "When Cherie called me two weeks ago and said Marissa was in an accident, all I could think about was that I'd given her up. Not only to be raised by another man, but I'd given up the opportunity to have any place in her life."

"Did she call because she thought Marissa wasn't going to make it?" Savvy leaned forward, resting her arms against her thighs as she spoke.

Brodie could see the concern in her eyes, and he was glad that he'd decided to tell her the truth. In high school, they'd confided in each other about everything. When she'd gone to Florida, and then he'd gone to UT, that had stopped. He'd continued that kind of relationship with Willow until they'd crossed the line and he'd left her. And he'd never had that kind of relationship, or friendship, with anyone since. At this moment, Brodie realized with complete clarity how very large a void that had been in his life.

"That's the thing," he rasped. "She was unconscious when they airlifted her to the hospital. Ryan and Cherie were told by the EMTs that they wouldn't know the extent of the injuries until she got to the hospital. Ryan and Cherie didn't know whether she'd make it or not."

"So the only reason they called you is because they thought she might die."

He nodded. "If that hadn't been the case, they wouldn't have called. And I can't pretend that I deserved to be called. I haven't been there. I'll be honest, I wasn't even sure how old Marissa was now when Cherie made that call."

"How old *is* she?" Savvy asked.

"Fifteen," he said. "Hard to believe. I've blown fifteen years." He shook his head. "I've messed up a lot during that time. And one of the biggest mistakes was with Willow." He looked away from Savvy and focused on the trees surrounding the trailer, the path that Dylan took when he wanted to get away. Brodie was tempted to get up right now and start down that same path, because walking away would be easier than admitting his mistakes. But walking away, from Cherie and from Willow and from every other potential commitment in his life, was what had caused his problems. He wouldn't do it again. "I told Cherie I wanted to have a relationship with Marissa. Some small part in her life."

"And what did she say?"

"She reminded me that I'd terminated my rights thirteen years ago. She said that Marissa deserved someone better than a thirty-three-year-old ladies' man who acted as if he was still in high school. Said my entire existence revolved around baseball, partying and women, not necessarily in that order."

Savvy audibly exhaled, the faintest of sounds, but because she leaned forward, her face close to his, Brodie heard. "Was she right?" she asked. "That your entire existence revolved around those things?"

"Yeah, she was. But that night at the hospital, I asked Cherie to forgive me for the mistakes I'd made. And I promised God and Cherie that I could change," he said, still staring at the woods instead of at Savvy. "I'm working hard to do that by helping those kids in the mentorship program at the college and by helping Dylan. I've started praying again, and I mean the words I pray. I've started back to church. And I've stopped the partying..." He paused. "And everything else."

They were silent for a moment, and then Savvy said, "The 'everything else'—that would include things like kissing me?"

He thought he heard a smile in her words, and he shifted on the step so that he could look up at her. Sure enough, those brown eyes sparkled, and an easy smile played with her pretty mouth. "Yeah, it would," he said, and wondered what God thought about the fact that even as he proclaimed that kissing her would be a mistake, he wanted to kiss her.

Forgive me, Lord.

She bobbed her head in one of those "yeah, I get it motions" he often got from his players. "You did the right thing," she said.

Brodie didn't know if she meant he did the right thing by apologizing to Cherie, or by stopping the partying, or by not kissing Savvy. But in his mind, he did the right thing with all of the above, so he wouldn't ask for clarification. Instead he just said, "Thanks."

Savvy hadn't anticipated Brodie sharing so much with her today, or how much she would feel toward him, especially since he'd left his daughter the same way her mother had left her. But in spite of initially seeing him as a terrible person for leaving his little girl, after listening to his story, she realized that he'd done the right thing by allowing Ryan to adopt Marissa. Brodie hadn't been ready to be a parent at the time, and Ryan obviously loved Cherie and Marissa.

But Savvy also saw that Brodie wanted to do the right thing now. This wasn't an act or a game. He meant the words he said. "I think you need to let Cherie know what all you're doing now. Did you tell her about helping the kids through the college mentor program? And did you tell her about Dylan? Because if she realizes how much you've changed, maybe she could tell Marissa. Chances are that your daughter would be more likely to listen to her mom than you," she said. "No offense."

The surprise on his face told her that he hadn't expected her to understand. He'd expected her to lash out and hate him, because of her own past. Or maybe because of the distance the two of them had experienced since high school. But Savvy knew the truth; that distance had started when she turned her back on him, not the other way around.

"None taken," he said. "And yeah, I told her, or I tried to."

"Then she'll figure it out, hopefully sooner rather than later."

The bus brakes sounded in the distance, and they both turned their attention toward the driveway, where the kids would make an appearance soon.

"Thank you," he mumbled, his words delivered

quickly, as if he needed to rush through them while he had a chance, and before the kids arrived. "For listening and for understanding."

Savvy couldn't wait any longer to tell him what she'd realized over the past few days, ever since she'd walked into that principal's office and faced Micca. She desperately wanted the school principal to forgive her for the mistakes of her past, but Micca had no reason at all to believe that Savvy had changed. Savvy hoped to show her that she had, over the next few weeks, as she worked with Rose and Daisy to improve their grades and as she tried to be a good mother figure in the girls' lives.

No, Micca hadn't seen that yet from Savvy. However, everything Savvy had seen and heard from Brodie since he'd followed her to the trailer last week told her that he had indeed changed. And she didn't want him wondering about how she felt. "I believe you."

His relief was obvious. "About…"

"About the fact that you're trying to change. And I believe that Willow probably wrote to you because she had forgiven you for what happened. Yes, I think she wanted you to help Dylan with school, but she wouldn't have asked you for help if she still hated you for what happened." The more Savvy thought about it, the more she knew it was true. "Willow had started back to church.

She'd found her faith again, and she'd found the ability to forgive."

For a moment, he sat there, looking at Savvy as though he wasn't quite sure he'd heard her correctly. Then he closed his eyes, and Savvy considered the possibility that he was praying. And if that action didn't make her think he'd asked for guidance from above, his next words did.

"How about you, Savvy? Do you forgive me?"

Did she? Savvy believed that he was trying to change. But forgiving him? Even now, she recalled the pain in Willow's voice when she'd finally told Savvy what he'd done to her. How he'd broken her heart. And though Willow had found her faith again, Savvy hadn't. Wasn't sure she ever would.

Because there were more pains in her past besides the loss of Brodie's friendship. And she had another man to forgive besides Brodie. Savvy wasn't ready to forgive that man, and didn't forgiving mean you wouldn't blame someone for that sin? So every now and then, Savvy would think about Willow, alone in that hotel room. And she'd blame Brodie all over again.

"Do you, Savvy?" he asked gruffly.

She wouldn't lie. "I don't know."

The twins bounded toward the trailer so that she didn't have to keep looking at the disappointment on Brodie's face.

"Aunt Savvy! We had a good day, and we didn't move our sticks," Rose said.

"And Mrs. Carter asked for readers at story time, and we both read a story from our new Bible storybooks," Daisy said.

"You took those to school?" Savvy asked in surprise. She hadn't seen the girls put them in their backpacks, but they had been carrying the books everywhere since they got them last week and learned that they were a gift from their mother.

"Yes," Rose said. "The words are ones we know, mostly."

Savvy nodded. "That's great, Rose." The books did include quite a few of their sight words. There were also some difficult words. "And you read the story okay?"

"Mrs. Carter said we did great!" Daisy said. Then she scooted past Brodie and Savvy. "Watch, Mr. Brodie." Pointing from one index card to the other, she read, "Red bag. Flowerpot."

Then Rose joined in. "Door. Step. Window."

"That's terrific," Brodie said, but Savvy noticed he didn't sound as enthusiastic as she'd have expected. Probably because she hadn't been able to say she forgave him.

But Savvy wouldn't say something she didn't mean. And for now, it wouldn't be true.

"What's in the red bag?" Rose asked, peeking in the tote Laura had given Savvy yesterday.

"It's another book for Dylan. Miss Laura gave it to me yesterday at the bookstore. I forgot to give it to him when he got in last night, so I put it out here so I would remember."

"Oh, okay. Can we get a snack?" Rose asked.

"Sure," Savvy said, and the girls wasted no time heading inside.

"Another book?" Dylan asked, nearing the porch.

Savvy grabbed the tote and handed it over. "Your mother had ordered it, and it just came in."

Dylan pulled the book out of the tote. *Daily Devotions for Teens*. "Something, huh? After what you said last night," he said to Brodie.

Savvy looked from Dylan to Brodie. "What did you say?"

"Dylan told me about his mom taking them to church, said that they had just started attending again, but that he thought going meant a lot to her," Brodie answered, then turned to Dylan. "You didn't ask your aunt Savvy about it yet?"

He shook his head. "I forgot." Dylan flipped through the book and said, "But she wanted us to go, and I kind of think we should, since that's what she wanted."

Savvy had thought the books from Willow, the Bibles and the devotional, would comfort Dylan and the girls, remind them that their mother loved them and cared about them. She should've realized that the gifts might cause them to want to return to church again. "I haven't gone to church in…" She didn't even know exactly how long. "In a very long time."

Dylan didn't miss a beat. "Coach Brodie said he'd take us."

"But you could go with us," Brodie offered, deliberately meeting her gaze.

Savvy had just told Brodie she didn't know if she could forgive him. If he knew the whole story, he'd realize that the church here in Claremont, and what had happened there so long ago, was the main reason she couldn't. "No," she said. "But you can take the kids. I'm sure that's what Willow would've wanted."

"Okay, I will," he said, looking slightly disappointed. And then he turned to Dylan. "Did you still want to hike up the mountain and do our studying at one of the cliffs?"

"Yeah," the boy said. "Just let me go grab something to eat. You want anything? We've got some protein bars that are pretty good."

"Nah, thanks."

Dylan stepped past Savvy and went inside, leaving her alone with Brodie and feeling incredibly awkward.

"I'll take them to the Wednesday-night service tomorrow," Brodie said. "If that's okay."

"It's fine."

He stood there a moment, and when Dylan didn't make a rapid appearance, he asked, "Savvy, what changed?"

"With what?"

"You. You never were big on church, but you went. And I don't remember you having a problem with forgiving folks back then, whenever Willow or I did something to tick you off. But you clearly do now. Why? What's this really all about?"

She remained silent, not willing to bring that horrible memory to light.

He still sat on the step below, and he edged up to put his face mere inches from hers. "I told you about my past. I've come completely clean, and you said you believed me."

"I do," she said emotionally.

"Don't you think I deserve the same thing? For you to tell me what happened with you back then?"

"It's...complicated."

"Complicated, how? Willow and I never knew why you took off to Florida, or what happened once you were there. But I'm pretty sure that your past, and especially what happened to you during those years, affects you today as much or more as mine." He reached out and gently stroked her hair, his eyes full of tenderness. "And let me tell you, your life will be a whole lot better if you get things right with whomever you did wrong, and if you get things right with God."

The door of the trailer banged against the side as Dylan hurried out. "Ready to go?" he asked.

"Yeah," Brodie said, withdrawing his hand and slowly standing up.

Savvy watched them as they turned toward the path and disappeared into the woods, neither of them looking back as they walked away. And all she could think about was how Brodie had it backward. She didn't have to get things right with someone she'd done wrong.

She'd been the one done wrong.

Chapter Ten

"Savvy, someone is here to see you," her grandmother called from the front of the store. "I'll bring him back."

Savvy had been in the stockroom since she arrived this morning, and she only had an hour before she'd need to leave and get home for the kids. Her clothes clung to her, not because they were too tight, but because the stockroom was like a sauna, and she'd been working nonstop sorting through a new shipment of camping gear. She hadn't wanted to run the air conditioner when she was the only one working in the back, but as she tucked another damp blond lock behind her ear, she second-guessed her decision to forgo AC to cut costs.

Suddenly, her stomach knotted. What if the "him" on his way back was Brodie?

For the past two weeks, he'd barely said hello

to her when he showed up at the trailer to work with Dylan. And the more he remained quiet, the more Savvy missed talking to him. She'd sensed them getting closer, the way they'd been in high school, when they talked about his past—and the fact that he'd nearly kissed her. But then he'd had to go and start talking about forgiveness and faith, subjects that'd been off-limits in Savvy's book for over a decade.

She couldn't forgive. And she'd lost her faith. Both for the same reason, and because of the same man.

Savvy, what changed?

Brodie's question haunted her, because the answer was simple.

Everything.

However, since she hadn't responded or explained, Brodie hadn't said more than a handful of words to her since. Even when he'd taken the kids to church on Wednesday nights and Sundays, he'd conversed more with Rose and Daisy than with Savvy. And he and Dylan were quickly becoming best buds, with Dylan passing his weekly reading tests at school and, from what she gathered from the teenager, doing very well on the baseball field, too. Truth be told, Savvy expected all of the kids to pass their standardized tests next week, and while she could take credit for helping Rose and Daisy, the reason Dylan had progressed so quickly had nothing to do with Savvy and everything to do with Brodie.

Savvy felt she should thank him, but he hadn't given her the chance, since he'd been talking to everyone in her household *except* Savvy. What if he'd come here because he'd finally decided he wanted to talk again, and she looked like death warmed over? She glanced in the full-length mirror covering the outside of the nearest closet. Yep, as bad as she feared. Hair yanked up in a messy ponytail. No makeup. Faded gray T-shirt. Army-green capris. Old tennis shoes with no laces. And no socks.

Don't be Brodie. Don't be Brodie. Don't be Brodie.

She continued the silent mantra until her grandmother entered the stockroom, and Savvy saw the man walking behind her.

And she suddenly wished it *had* been Brodie.

"I'll leave you two to talk," her grandmother said, smiling at Savvy before turning and leaving the two of them alone.

"Savvy, I'd hoped to see you at church with the children," Brother Henry said. "It's been a long time, and I wanted to visit, see how you're doing."

Savvy hadn't seen the preacher from her youth since she left Claremont the summer she graduated from high school. He'd aged well, his hair lightening to a snowy white that seemed to showcase the kindness in his blue eyes. But she'd often wondered if this man might be the only person in Claremont who knew why she left. "Hello, Brother Henry," she replied.

He nodded toward one of the old chairs in the stockroom, the seat fabric nearly threadbare and duct tape holding the armrest in place. "May I sit down?"

Savvy nodded. "Of course." She didn't hear any accusation in his tone, but then again, he'd never been that kind of preacher. Brother Henry focused on grace and love more than fire and brimstone. But still, if he knew why Savvy went to Florida, she'd expect to hear something to that effect in his tone. Disappointment. Or disapproval. She heard neither.

He took a seat in the chair, easing into it as though testing whether it could hold his weight. He wasn't overly heavy, but the chair was in rough shape. He nodded when it held firm. "Like I said, I'd hoped to see you at church with Willow's children. I'm glad Brodie is bringing them, but I do think it'd benefit them to have you there, too."

He gave her the gentle smile she remembered him offering throughout her teens, the one that said he cared about her and that he felt sorry for her losing her mother the way she did. It touched her heart then, and that hadn't changed. "I believe it'd benefit you, too, to come back to church, Savvy. We have a congregation that's loving and supportive, a lot of the same members we had when you left, and they'd appreciate the opportunity to help you with anything you need. I hope you know that."

Savvy felt a bead of sweat trickle from her neck down the center of her shirt, and she wondered if it was because of the heat in the stockroom or how uncomfortable she was with this conversation. Since Brother Henry didn't seem to be sweltering, she assumed the latter.

In any event, Savvy needed this discussion to end, and the only way to do that was to tell him the truth. "I don't think I can come back."

He nodded as though he had expected her answer, which only led credence to the possibility that he knew the truth. "Well, I wanted you to know we'd like to have you, and I wanted to extend a personal invitation for you to come this Sunday. I think you'll really enjoy the lesson I'm preparing."

Savvy didn't want to know what kind of lesson he thought she'd enjoy, so she simply said, "I appreciate the invitation."

He sighed, then pushed up from the chair. "I'd like to see you there, Savvy. A lot of people would, including your grandparents. And I'm sure it'd mean a lot to Dylan, Rose and Daisy."

She swallowed. "Thanks again for the invitation."

He touched the back of the chair. "I think it's nice when people still see the usefulness in things that have been through a hard time. Sometimes they just need a chance," he said, and then he turned and left Savvy to wonder just how much he knew.

He'd barely cleared the doorway to the front of the store when her phone rang. She glanced at the display and didn't recognize the number. "Hello?"

"Hey, it's me." Brodie had rarely spoken to her in the past two weeks, and he'd never called her cell, so naturally, her heart fluttered at the sound of his voice. She wanted to ask why he was calling now, find out if something had changed, but instead she just said, "Hi."

"I wanted to let you know that I'm picking the kids up when they get off the bus today and taking them somewhere for a little while, so if you need to work late, or want to do something after you get off work, that's fine."

She frowned. "You realize you didn't ask me if you could take them anywhere."

"That's because I can't tell you where I'm taking them. It's a surprise, and it was Dylan's idea. So just trust me."

Trust him. Oddly enough, Savvy realized that she did. "Okay. But don't keep them out too late. And will they be home for dinner?"

"I thought we'd pick something up. Want us to bring you something?"

All of this conversation from him surprised her, but she wouldn't question it. She liked chatting with him again, especially about the kids. "No, I'll fix myself something at home. But thanks."

"Okay. Enjoy your afternoon," he said, and then hung up.

Leaving Savvy to wonder not only what the preacher had been up to, but what Brodie was up to, as well.

After work, she went home and showered, tidied up and then headed toward town. It felt odd not having the kids to take care of, cook for, help with homework and do every other daily activity that had consumed her world since she arrived in Claremont. She'd have thought that having an "afternoon off" would appeal to her, but she found herself continually wondering how Dylan was doing with his baseball. Today was his scheduled practice day with Brodie, and she was certain Brodie wouldn't have changed that. And when they were practicing, what were the girls doing? If they were at the playground, was Brodie able to watch them while he helped Dylan? What if they wanted something to drink, or had to use the bathroom?

She decided to pass by Hydrangea Park on her way to town, just in case they were there and Brodie needed her help. Sure enough, she spotted his truck near the baseball field where he and Dylan practiced. Instead of driving down closer to the field, Savvy parked in the lot that overlooked the complex and watched.

The girls weren't on the playground, but were in the outfield, one in right field and one in left. They each had on a small baseball cap that she hadn't seen before, and she noticed they both had gloves as well, though Rose was currently tossing hers in the air and trying to catch it. Dylan was at the plate, and Brodie was pitching.

She watched him throw a pitch Dylan's way, and the boy, in a stance that reminded her of the way Brodie had batted in high school, hit an impressive line drive over second and then started running toward first. Rose and Daisy both looked at the ball heading into the outfield, and they took off running to get it while Dylan started toward second.

Savvy then saw Brodie, running as fast as he could toward the outfield. But he didn't head toward the ball. Instead he scooped up Rose in one arm, then darted across the field to get Daisy in the other, and then the three of them ran toward the fence to get the ball. He tilted Daisy to the ground, and she grabbed it, and then they ran toward home plate, the girls' mouths wide-open with their laughter, and Dylan also whooping with joy as he passed third base.

The Brodie-Rose-Daisy trio crossed the plate just after Dylan, and then they all fell on the ground laughing, with Brodie tickling Rose and Daisy...and shoving playful punches at Dylan.

Savvy's hand moved to her throat. Her heart pulled solidly in her chest. This...was what a real family looked like.

She wanted to join in, but Brodie had said they were doing something that was a surprise. Evidently, that would come after they finished Dylan's practice. She didn't want to spoil the surprise, and she didn't want to join in when he hadn't invited her. But as she drove away, she couldn't deny a heavy sadness settling over her soul.

She'd always wanted to be a part of a real family.

Brodie wrote the word *wood* on a Post-it note and slapped it on the pile in the bed of his truck.

"Wood!" Rose and Daisy yelled together, clapping because they knew they had the right answer.

"Very good," Brodie said while Dylan wrote *bucket*, *paint* and *brush* on three more Post-its and placed them on the corresponding items, also in the bed of the truck.

"Bucket!" Daisy said.

"Paint!" Rose followed.

"Brush!" they yelled together.

Granted, Brodie knew that they got many of the words because they knew the items with the Post-its, but he suspected they were still learning, which was the entire point of this game. He'd started this afternoon at the baseball field, continued through their dinner and this shopping trip and planned to keep it up tomorrow when they worked at the trailer. "Okay, time to climb in and head back to see Aunt Savvy."

"And tell her about her surprise?" Daisy asked.

"Yep, and about how we're going to be studying while we work, right?" Brodie said, buckling them in the backseat while Dylan sat in the front.

"This is pretty cool," the teenager said, holding the tape measure Brodie had purchased for him at the building supply store. "Because our place is finally gonna be fixed up, and we're studying without really studying."

Brodie climbed in and grinned. "That's the plan." And he was proud of the fact that he had come up with the idea on his own. He'd also been happy to give Savvy the afternoon off, since she'd been working or taking care of the kids 24/7 since she'd arrived in Claremont. Truth was, he'd wanted to do something for her, particularly this weekend, and even though he'd been annoyed at her unwillingness to forgive him, he'd decided to move past that for now. This was a big weekend for the kids and Savvy, too.

Their first Mother's Day without their mom, and Savvy's first Mother's Day as acting mom. Brodie knew the potential for a lot of sadness could occur, so he'd jumped right on board when Dylan suggested they do something for Savvy this weekend, because she was "like a mother" to them now. Dylan's words, not Brodie's. But those words had touched Brodie's heart, and he'd known exactly what they could do. The fact that he could also help the kids study for next week's standardized achievement tests made the idea even better.

By the time they pulled up at the trailer, it was almost dark, and Brodie saw Savvy climbing out of her truck. Good, she'd taken his advice and spent time on her own. He parked, and the kids hurriedly climbed out, all of them eager to tell her about their afternoon.

"We played baseball!" Rose exclaimed, running toward Savvy.

"And we ate chicken fingers for dinner," Daisy said.

"And we read lots and lots of words," Rose continued. "See?" She pointed at the Post-its that covered practically every item inside the truck. A few remained on the items in the truck bed, too, and Savvy seemed to examine all of them as she neared.

"Wow," she said. "Y'all had a busy afternoon."

Brodie glanced toward her and was surprised at the way the scene hit him, as if he were the father returning home from taking the kids, and Savvy, the mother in this scenario, marveled at all they'd done.

He liked the image. A lot.

"We're gonna fix up the trailer tomorrow," Dylan told her. "Coach Brodie and I will keep putting words on everything to help Rose and Daisy get ready for their test, and he got me this." He held up the tape measure. "So I can measure stuff and then add and subtract the fractions while we work. So I'll be ready for my test, too." Dylan's excitement was evident, and Brodie saw in Savvy's eyes that she realized it as much as he did.

"Dylan, that's awesome," she said.

Dylan grinned, then looked at Brodie. "You want me to start unloading the back?"

"Sure," Brodie answered.

"We'll help. Okay, Dylan?" Rose asked.

"Yeah, there are some things you can carry," Dylan said. "Like the brushes and stuff."

"Okay!" the girls said in unison, and followed their brother to the back of the truck.

Savvy had been on the passenger's side, and she walked around the front to be near Brodie.

He had been so eager to hear the kids tell her about their day that he hadn't really looked at her since they arrived. But now, as she came close, he couldn't stop. She wore a sleeveless white blouse, peach shorts and sparkly sandals. Her hair looked lighter and had more of those wispy strands curling toward her face. She had some kind of shimmery peach shadow on her eyes and a matching gloss on her lips.

She even smelled like peaches, and Brodie took an extradeep breath to simply enjoy it.

"Wow," he said, and welcomed the blush that his assessment brought to her cheeks.

"I haven't had a chance to get my hair done since I moved back, so I went to the Cut and Curl, and Ruth Ellen Riley worked me in." She smiled toward the kids, helping each other unload the smaller items from the truck. "Ruth Ellen also had a new makeup line she was trying out, and she tested the colors out on me."

"I like it," Brodie said, as if she didn't already know that by the fact that he couldn't take his eyes off her.

She lowered her voice to a whisper. "The ladies there were very nice to me. They said they'd heard about how well the kids were doing." She ran a hand down Rose's pigtail as she passed the truck carrying a box of nails toward the deck. "I almost didn't go to the hair salon, because I wasn't sure, you know, how the women would be."

"Whether they'd treat you badly because of what happened in high school?" he asked.

"Yeah. But they were great."

"So those you hurt back then have forgiven you?" he asked, and immediately knew that wasn't the right thing to say. They were talking again, and he shouldn't mess that up.

But she didn't cut him off this time. Instead she answered, "I guess they have."

"Coach Brodie, can you help me with the wood?" Dylan asked.

Brodie nodded. "Sure thing."

"Okay if I help, too?" Savvy asked, stepping toward the back of the truck.

"You look mighty nice to be unloading wood. This'll probably get you dirty," Brodie warned as he and Dylan carried a couple of two-by-fours toward the trailer to start a stack for tomorrow's work.

She moved to the back of the truck, lifted the end of another two-by-four and waited for Brodie to help. "I don't care about that," she said. "I really want to be a part of this, too."

He grabbed the other end and gave her a smile. "Then, I wouldn't have it any other way."

Chapter Eleven

Savvy dropped, exhausted, to the new deck and laid back to peer at the dark blue sky. The sweet scent of sawdust coupled with fresh paint filled the air, and every muscle in her body ached.

She couldn't remember the last time she'd felt this happy.

"It's incredible," Dylan said to Brodie as they tossed the discarded pieces of wood in the back of Brodie's truck. "I can't believe how much we did in a day."

"Me, either," Brodie said. "Of course, it helped that Titus Jameson stopped by to see how we were doing."

"Yeah. I've met him at church, I think, but I didn't know he did construction stuff. He builds houses?"

Brodie nodded. "That's what he does."

"Kinda cool that he came by just after seeing us at the building supply store, huh?"

"That's the neat thing about people around here," Brodie remarked. "They like helping each other out."

"Maybe he'll help us again, whenever we build a house here," Dylan said.

Savvy leaned up to hear Brodie's response. Dylan had already started including Brodie in his plans for the future, and she wasn't certain whether he wanted to be included, beyond helping Dylan with those tests this week.

"Maybe he will," Brodie said, smiling at the teenager and looking as though he meant every word.

Savvy wasn't surprised that Dylan wanted Brodie around. The two had bonded over the past few weeks, and she was glad for it. Willow's son needed a male figure in his life, and Brodie had done an amazing job fitting the bill.

But did Brodie plan on sticking around solely for Dylan, or was he thinking about staying involved for Savvy, too?

As if he knew her thoughts, Brodie glanced toward the deck and winked at her.

Savvy grinned. Like a love-struck high schooler. But she couldn't help it. The entire scenario this weekend, of finding Brodie willing to talk to her again, and then seeing him with the kids on the field last night, and spending the whole day with them today... All of it gave this thirty-three-year old a mammoth-size crush on the handsome baseball coach.

And it also made her realize that she'd been too hard on him. She'd suspected that he'd changed, but over the past few weeks, and especially this weekend, she had no doubt. And he wanted her forgiveness.

She planned to let him know he had it. But she also owed him the explanation of why she had such a difficult time forgiving.

He'd trusted her enough to tell her about his past. Tonight, somehow, she'd tell him about hers. And she prayed he wouldn't leave and want nothing to do with her anymore after he heard.

A loud vehicle coming up the driveway caused her to sit up on the deck. It was nearly dark. The only person who came this late was Brodie, when he brought Dylan home after baseball practice. But he was already here, tossing the last bits of wood in the truck with Dylan. Rose and Daisy had given up working outside and were watching cartoons while they waited on Dylan, Brodie and Savvy to come inside.

Savvy's grandfather beeped the horn in their car as he and her grandmother drove up. Savvy could see her grandmother through the front windshield, and she pointed at the trailer, her mouth moving a mile a minute as she apparently told her husband what she thought of the changes.

Savvy grinned, glad they had come to visit. Jolaine had called earlier, and Savvy informed her that they were all working on fixing up the trailer. Obviously, her grandparents had decided to see the finished product.

"Oh, my, it's amazing what all of you got done!" her grandmother exclaimed, climbing out of the car and moving toward the deck.

"Nice job, guys," Savvy's grandfather said to Brodie and Dylan.

"We worked all day long," Dylan said. "And just finished."

"Well, you'd better not let too many people see this, or they'll start calling you for all of their home-improvement projects," he said. "Why, we should bring Titus Jameson out here from Jameson Construction. I'd bet even he'd be impressed, and he does top-notch work."

"He came out and saw it already," Dylan told the older man. "We ran into him when we bought the wood, and he wanted to come see if we needed any help."

James Bowers nodded. "Yep, that's the way folks are around here. Nice, isn't it?"

"It sure is," Brodie answered.

"I can't believe you did all of this in one day," Jolaine said to Dylan and Brodie. "It's amazing."

"We had to finish it today," Dylan explained.

That was news to Savvy. Why did they have to finish in a day?

Her grandmother wondered the same thing. "Why's that, Dylan?" she asked.

"Because tomorrow's Mother's Day," Dylan said. "And we were doing it because it's something my mom always wanted, and because we thought Aunt Savvy would like it, since she's, you know, taking care of us now."

Savvy bit the inside of her lip to keep it from trembling. Blinked a couple of times. Then she swallowed and said, "Thank you, Dylan."

He nodded. "We couldn't have done it if Coach Brodie hadn't helped. But we did."

"You sure did," Savvy's grandfather said, putting an arm around Dylan. "Good job, son."

"Thanks."

"Well, then, we picked a perfect night to take the kids to celebrate, since they did so much today," Jolaine said.

"Celebrate?" Dylan asked.

"Yeah, we saw one of those big carnival things set up over in Stockville and thought we'd take you kids, if you want," James replied. "Or are you too big for carnivals now?"

"I like carnivals," Dylan said with a grin. "Especially the roller coaster and the bullet ride."

"Bullet ride?" Jolaine asked.

"The ones that look like a bullet and take you upside down over and over," Dylan explained.

"Are you okay to ride that one on your own?" she asked worriedly.

Dylan laughed. "Yeah, or you could ride it with me." He pointed to Savvy's grandfather.

"I might just do that," he said, causing Savvy to laugh.

"You want to see if the girls would like to come?" her grandmother queried.

"Sure," Savvy said. She climbed up from the deck and then opened the door. "Rose, Daisy, do y'all want to go to the carnival with my grandparents?"

A dual yelling of "Yes!" echoed from the house, and within seconds, the girls were on the deck ready to go.

"That'd be a yes," Savvy said wryly.

Rose and Daisy hugged her as they passed.

"Bye, Aunt Savvy," Rose said, and Daisy followed.

"Y'all have fun," Savvy murmured.

"Hang on. I'm gonna go change clothes, and then I'll be ready." Dylan started toward the trailer but stopped to view the remaining tools on the deck. "Or do you want me to help you pick those up first?" he asked Brodie.

"No, you go ahead and have fun," Brodie said. "I've got this."

"Great!" Dylan headed into the house while the girls played on the swing set and her grandfather helped Brodie gather tools.

Savvy's grandmother sat beside her on the step. "You know," she said, barely above a whisper, "that's a good man, right there."

Savvy grinned. "I love how you still talk about Granddaddy that way."

Her grandmother laughed. "Oh, well, he's a good one, too, but you and I both know I was talking about Brodie Evans. I'm not sure what happened to you two over the years, or why you drifted apart, but let me tell you that seeing you and Brodie together, and watching the way you both care about these kids… It does wonderful things to my heart."

Savvy silently agreed. It did wonderful things to her heart, too.

"For the past few years, Savvy, I kept praying that one day you'd call and say you met someone nice, someone good. Someone who you thought you could spend your life with. That never happened, and I wondered why. But now I know." She pointed toward her husband and Brodie, chatting as they reorganized everything in the back of the truck. "God had this one waiting for you."

"I think you may be reading too much into things," Savvy said. Though she silently wondered whether it might be true.

"I don't think so, but we'll see, won't we?" her grandmother answered.

Dylan emerged from the trailer, and Savvy caught a familiar masculine scent as he passed between the two of them on the steps. He'd changed from his T-shirt and cutoff jeans to a collared shirt and almost-new jeans. He'd also put on a pair of hiking boots similar to the ones Brodie typically wore.

"I'm ready," he said, to no one in particular. "Y'all ready to go?"

"I believe someone might be trying to catch the attention of the opposite sex," her grandmother whispered in Savvy's ear. "And he's a cutie, too. You're gonna have to keep an eye on him."

Savvy groaned. She didn't know if she was prepared for raising a teenage boy, but she didn't have a choice, did she? It had started. Dylan was definitely dressing to catch attention, and her grandmother was right: he was a cutie. She hoped she made it through these years okay.

Brodie grinned at Dylan. "You going to the carnival or on a date?" he asked, expressing the same sentiment Savvy and her grandmother had kept to themselves.

Dylan shrugged and grinned back, and Savvy noticed his dimples popping into place with the action. She supposed she hadn't seen him smile enough over the past few weeks to really see them, but she did now. And she liked seeing him smile.

"Okay, kids, let's load up!" her grandfather yelled.

Rose and Daisy darted from the swing set to their car and climbed in. Dylan followed. He looked even older than thirteen when he got in the backseat next to his sisters, and Savvy appreciated the way he helped them buckle up and said something to the two of them that made them laugh. He was a good big brother, and she was glad for that. She'd always wanted a big brother or sister. But she'd had Brodie and Willow, and back then, they had been all she'd needed.

She waved goodbye as her grandparents and the kids started down the driveway.

"We'll be back before the sun comes up!" her grandfather called out his window, and the entire carload laughed.

Brodie had finished putting everything in the truck, and he also waved at them leaving before he walked over to sit beside Savvy on the deck.

Savvy inhaled, then turned to him and asked, "Did you give Dylan some of your aftershave, or whatever that is?"

He grinned. "He wanted something to make him smell manly. That's what he told me. And so I gave him a bottle of the cologne I wear."

She nodded. "I smelled it when he headed out."

"And I'm guessing you don't mind the scent?"

"No, I don't mind it," she said softly. She liked it, in fact. A lot. But on Dylan, it was cute. A teenager trying to be grown. On Brodie, it was…intriguing. A man emphasizing the fact that he was all male. Yes, she definitely liked it.

They sat there for a moment in silence, each of them scanning the new deck, awning, steps and skirting that they'd all worked on today. The exhaustion was totally worth it, because the place looked so much better.

"I really appreciate everything you did this weekend," she said.

"We all did it," he corrected.

"Yeah, but you went and got all of the materials." She lifted one of the Post-it notes from the deck. "And you made it a learning lesson for the girls and for Dylan. I was so impressed with the way he added and subtracted those fractions when y'all measured the wood."

"Their standardized tests are this week, right?" Brodie asked.

"Monday," she said.

"That's what I thought. I didn't want to waste a day of reviewing, and this way, we were able to finish the Mother's Day gift Dylan wanted to give at the same time."

"I still can't believe he thought of that," she

murmured. "He tries to act tough, but he's got a sentimental heart."

"He does. And he thinks a lot of you, Savvy, and everything you do to take care of him and his sisters. He told me that, when he asked me about fixing up the trailer."

"Thanks," she said. "I needed to hear that." She thought about all of the materials and supplies they'd used throughout the day and looked over at him. "But you need to tell me how much you spent on all of this. Those supplies aren't cheap, and I don't want you footing the bill for something that benefits me."

"It benefits you and the kids, and I wanted to do it," he said, and before she could resume her argument, he added, "A star in my crown, remember?"

Savvy gave up. "I remember, and I won't fight you on it. But I hope you know how grateful I am. I got nervous every time I thought about what might be living under the trailer with all of that broken skirting. And the rain pouring through the awning spooked me whenever it'd storm."

Brodie eyed the new awning. "I didn't like the rain coming through there either, but that isn't what spooks you during storms. You haven't liked them ever since that big one on the day you found out your mother had died. And that's understandable." He turned toward her. "You see storms as something to be afraid of, not just because they're scary, but because you got the worst news of your life during a storm."

He stated the truth without questioning any of it, and Savvy couldn't deny it. Brodie had seen her through all of those storms during high school, each time she'd been terrified to learn someone else had died, and so he understood, really understood, her fear.

"I don't know how I'd have made it through all that back then without you," she admitted.

He eased closer to her on the step, his shoulder brushing hers as he leaned toward her ear. "You trusted me…back then."

Savvy heard the disappointment in his voice, and she couldn't hold back telling him how her feelings had changed. "I trust you now, too, Brodie."

He exhaled, so close that she felt his breath against her neck, and then he eased away, bracing his elbows on the deck and leaning back as though contemplating whether he believed her words. After a moment, he said, "You'll trust me, but you won't forgive me."

He had no way of knowing why she'd had such a hard time trusting him, and especially forgiving him. The only way he'd know was if she told him everything. So she took a deep breath, said a little prayer and then hoped that God was listening, because she needed all the help she could get.

She'd kept this secret for so long that telling it felt like ripping a bandage off an unhealed wound.

But she'd do it. No matter how difficult or painful it was. She just had to gather her courage and find the right words.

Brodie had enjoyed everything about this weekend—spending time with the kids last night and then working with them and Savvy today to fix up the trailer. They'd felt like a family, and he'd loved every minute of it. He'd been certain Savvy had decided to let him in, be close to him again. They'd joked around all day, borderline flirting as they handed each other the tools or laughed with the kids. He felt their relationship evolving once more and had even regretted giving her the cold shoulder over the past couple of weeks after he'd gotten so irritated by her unwillingness to forgive.

Now she said she trusted him. But she wouldn't say she forgave him for what happened with Willow. Why couldn't she? And how could they have a relationship without her forgiveness?

Because the more he was around Savvy and the kids, the more he wanted a relationship. He wanted a family, but only if that family included Savvy. Yet she still seemed so stuck in the past and couldn't see beyond one of the worst mistakes of his life. He didn't know what else to do. "Savvy, I'm going to head on home. I'll come pick the kids up for church in the morning," he said, starting to get up from the deck.

She grabbed his wrist, tugged him back down. "Don't go, Brodie. Please. You told me about what happened to you back then, and I want—I need—to tell you what happened to me."

He sat back down beside her on the deck. The sky grew darker, but he could still see her face, and he could tell that whatever she wanted to say wasn't going to be easy, but he also knew that he wanted to hear it. "Okay," he said gently. "I'm listening."

She let go of his wrist and rubbed her palms against her thighs the way she often did when she was nervous or uncomfortable. Brodie wanted to ease her discomfort the way he had done in high school, by telling her everything would be okay. But since he didn't know what she was about to say, he couldn't in good conscience make that promise. He just prayed he'd respond in the appropriate way to whatever she revealed.

"That June after we graduated from high school…" she began.

Brodie nodded. "Before you left in July."

"Yeah. That June, in the middle of the month, the church had the summer revival. I don't know if they still have them, because I've purposely not asked my grandparents about them over the years, but that year they had one. It lasted a week, and they held it outside, under that huge red-and-white tent that they put up behind the church, on that big piece of land near the cemetery."

Brodie nodded. "I remember the revivals." But he had no idea how a revival could be the source of Savvy's unwillingness to go to church, or to forgive him for what he had done in the past.

"Yeah, that one was different for me."

He tried his best to remember that specific revival. Maybe the preacher had said something that upset Savvy. Maybe he'd talked about negligent parents, or said something else that corresponded to Savvy's childhood, and turned her away from God. But Brodie couldn't fathom what that would've been. "How was that one different?"

"The preacher's name was Calvin Morrell. He was known for his powerful sermons, and that summer, he traveled around the Southeast preaching at revivals. His son, Tyler, traveled with him as his assistant. Tyler made sure everything was set up correctly and basically did anything his father needed during each revival." She released a breath. "But he also spoke to the youth, specifically the teenagers, since he wasn't that much older and could still relate to teenagers."

"How old was he?" Brodie asked.

"Twenty-six," she said, "and I'd just turned eighteen," she quietly added.

Brodie nodded and finally latched on to the lost memory of the guy who'd intrigued all of the females that summer.

Savvy took a raspy breath. "At that time, Tyler thought he'd probably become a preacher, too, like his dad. He was younger than any preacher I'd heard before, but he was amazing. He had all of the teenagers on the edge of their seats, me included, and he made you feel like he had all the answers." She met his eyes briefly before looking away. "You know, like he was so smart, so clever with the analogies he gave in his sermons and the way he described life. There was something about him that was…mesmerizing."

Now that Brodie remembered the guy, he knew exactly which revival Savvy referred to, and he realized that he'd also been in the group listening. Savvy was right; Tyler Morrell had been different from any preacher Brodie had ever seen, too. He'd looked more like a collegiate athlete than a future preacher, and he'd had a confidence that even Brodie had envied. But Brodie also recalled another tidbit about that guy.

"Didn't y'all say it was a shame he wasn't available? Wasn't he married?" Brodie asked, thinking he might know what had happened back then. And he didn't like it at all. The thought of Savvy having an affair with a married man didn't sit well. Why hadn't she talked to Brodie about it?

Or Willow? They'd have steered her clear of that kind of mess, that kind of sin.

"He wasn't married," Savvy said. "Not yet."

"Not yet?" Brodie repeated.

"He was engaged," she said, still rubbing her hands against her thighs. "And on the last night he was here, after he finished speaking, the church had the dinner on the grounds. We had the biggest crowd ever, because everyone was so taken with him. People came from as far away as Atlanta to hear him speak."

Brodie nodded, again finding a brief recollection of the crowded tent, the casseroles lining endless tables and the entire church gathered together to share a meal. But he couldn't remember who he'd been with, whether he, Savvy and Willow had been together at the time. Right now, looking at Savvy's face, her jaw set firm and her eyes looking at the deck steps instead of at Brodie, he suspected she had been with the dashing young preacher. "I remember some of it," he said.

"I thought he was unique, like no one I'd met before. So I waited until he was alone, after most everyone had left for the night, and I went to talk to him, ask him about his plans, what he thought his future would be. Basically, I just wanted to know more about him…"

She stopped talking, and Brodie thought that might be all she was willing to tell, but then she said, "I kissed him, and I told him that maybe he wasn't with the right person. Maybe he hadn't met the right one when he asked her to marry him, and maybe he'd met the right one that night." She shook her head. "I remember it so well. He told me he'd taken a job in Panama City Beach working with a summer camp program his dad was starting. The job started the next week. I basically threw myself at him. I told him I'd always dreamed of living at the beach, and that I knew I could make him happier than anyone else. That he should take me along to Florida."

"Savvy, why? You didn't have it so bad here… and I thought you were happy. You were working at your grandparents' store and you'd talked about going to college in Stockville, but then you all of a sudden said you were going to Florida, and you wouldn't tell Willow or me what had changed."

"You had your scholarship to UT and were about to leave us, and Willow only wanted to meet someone, fall in love and stay in Claremont forever. I wanted to see the world, and at that time in my life, living at the beach seemed like perfection." She hitched in a breath. "But I knew if I told y'all I was going down there to be with him, with a guy engaged to someone else—and a preacher, no less—y'all would have talked me out of it."

"You've got that right," he bit out.

"But I didn't want to be talked out of it. I was

in love, or I thought I was. I remember telling him over and over that it was love at first sight. And he'd agreed."

Brodie was having a hard time making sense of it. "Willow and I never knew what happened to make you leave, and then we couldn't get in touch with you after you moved. You called every now and then, but you kept us in the dark." He clenched his jaw. "What happened, after you got there?"

"It was great, at first. He had a little rental house not too far from the beach, and we stayed there."

"So you were living with him," Brodie said.

"Not all the time," she answered. "He had his place, a little villa on the beach near the campsite, and that was where he and his wife were planning on living after they married. That was where I thought *I'd* live one day, when Ty broke up with her and married me. He told me he would. He was just waiting for the right time."

Brodie wanted to punch Tyler Morrell. In fact, it was a very good thing the guy lived six hours away. "How long did you live with him?"

"Nearly three years," she said hoarsely.

Brodie remembered those three years, the times that he and Willow had confided in each other, grown closer to each other, because they were missing the third link of their trio. And they'd gotten so close, in fact, that they'd crossed the line of friendship and ended up in bed. Not that he blamed Savvy for that; it had been totally his fault. But not having her around didn't help. And right now, if he really wanted to blame someone, it'd be Tyler Morrell.

Savvy rubbed her hand across her cheeks and Brodie realized she'd started crying. He hated that guy even more for making her cry after all this time.

"You remember how I always called myself the black sheep of the Bowers family?" she asked.

"Yeah," he said, never liking the nickname she'd bestowed upon herself.

"Well, that's what he called me. His little black sheep. He said I'd be his secret, until he gently broke up with her and then brought me out for the world to see. I'd be beside him in the pew at church one day, and we'd run that church camp and live in that pretty home."

Brodie remained silent while Savvy paused, apparently gathering the courage to continue.

She sniffed. "I couldn't wait. I envisioned my wedding. Willow would be a bridesmaid, and you would be a groomsman. My grandparents would be thrilled because I was marrying a guy I met at church who had plans to work with the church. A good guy." She laughed, but the sound was watery and weak.

The pain in her voice pierced his heart, and he eased closer to her on the deck, wrapping an arm around her as she continued.

"I was good enough to keep him entertained away from his church friends," she said. "I just wasn't good enough to be by his side in the pew. And when he finally told me that he'd decided that he really did love his fiancée, and that he was going to marry her, he said she was his white sheep. The *pure* one."

Plenty of words filled Brodie's thoughts about the preacher's boy, but saying them wouldn't do anything to help Savvy now, so he harnessed the anger and gave her what she needed, someone who would listen and understand.

Savvy shook her head. "That's what he said. I was the black sheep. She was the white. I was temporary love, but she was forever. He married her, and they're still together."

"How do you know? Don't tell me you stayed in touch with that jerk?"

She glanced at Brodie sheepishly. "I've looked them up on the internet a few times… I couldn't help it. They have two children, a boy and a girl. And their family picture is beautiful. Looks like a Christmas card. Tyler didn't stay working for the church, though. He started his own business selling real estate, beach property mostly." She took a deep breath, her shoulders lifting and then falling abruptly with the action. "Looks as if he's doing very well."

Everything fell into place, and Brodie understood why it was so hard for Savvy to trust a man again. Why it was nearly impossible for her to forgive. "And you gave up on loving a guy for life and lost your faith because of him. You blamed God."

She shrugged. "I don't know. I blamed Ty. But God seemed to keep protecting him, in spite of how much he hurt me. Tyler has everything I wanted. The family. The church. The house. God gave him everything, and He left me with nothing."

"Savvy, God wasn't the one who hurt you. Tyler was," Brodie said, brushing his hand along her hair. "And he was a fool to hurt you, not only emotionally, but spiritually."

"I know," she choked out.

Brodie wondered about something, and the only way to learn the answer was to ask. "Savvy, have you been with another man since then?"

She chewed on her lower lip, then shook her head. "No. Not even a kiss. I haven't trusted anyone enough to let him get that close. And I haven't needed anyone. I've been fine on my own."

"I'm so sorry for what you went through," he said, still soothingly rubbing his hand along her soft hair.

They sat in silence for a moment; then she whispered, "I haven't wanted to kiss anyone—" she tilted her head to look up at Brodie "—until that night when you nearly kissed me."

Brodie tenderly touched his fingertips to her temple then traced them along the smoothness of her face, until he cradled her chin. Her eyes were still moist from her tears, but she didn't show any fear. And this time, Brodie didn't stop at nearly.

Chapter Twelve

Savvy touched her lips and smiled, replaying the moment when Brodie had closed the distance between them, his mouth finding hers and every one of her fears dissipating as she lost herself in his arms. It'd been a long time since she'd wanted a man's kiss.

And she hadn't wanted that kiss with Brodie to end.

"Aunt Savvy, wake up." Tiny hands shoved at her side. "It's time to get up."

Savvy opened her eyes, wondered how many times she'd replayed that amazing kiss, and then smiled at the twins standing beside the bed. "Hey," she said, easing up on the pillow. "Good morning. Hang on, and I'll make your breakfast, okay?"

Daisy shook her head. "Nope," she said, and then she looked behind her, where Dylan entered the bedroom carrying a tray.

"Today *we* fixed breakfast. It's a special day," Rose declared.

Dylan nodded, then waited for Savvy to sit up in the bed before he placed the tray in front of her. The plate held two pieces of cinnamon toast and an apple. "We tried to make coffee, but it didn't turn out so good," he said. "So we've got juice."

"I'll get the juice," Rose offered, hurrying out of the room.

"I didn't want to carry the tray with the juice on it," Dylan said. "Wasn't sure I wouldn't spill it on the way in."

"That was probably smart," Savvy replied, looking at the breakfast before her, the children filling her room, already feeling her body stuffed...with love. How had she ever lived without them?

Daisy placed a small clay pot with *Aunt Savvy* painted on its side on the tray. A tiny pink flower centered the pot of dirt. Savvy smiled at the capital *A*'s. Daisy loved making capital *A*'s. Then Rose returned with a plastic Dora the Explorer cup half filled with orange juice and handed it over to Savvy.

Savvy placed the juice on the tray. "You fixed me breakfast?"

"For Mother's Day," Rose said. "Because our mommy went to heaven, and you take care of us now."

Savvy's eyes stung with unshed tears, but if she cried, the children might cry, too. And she didn't want to see them crying. Not today. Not ever. She touched her hand to Rose's cheek, and then Daisy's. "Thank you," she whispered.

"I made another flowerpot, too. It's for Mommy," Daisy said. "Mr. Brodie said we can take it when we go to church."

Savvy looked at Dylan. While the twins seemed excited about the breakfast presentation, he remained somber and quiet, even though he'd been the one to carry the tray. But then he noticed her looking at him, and he nodded and gave her a little smile. "We wanted to do something special today, something else besides the stuff we did yesterday."

"I appreciate this, Dylan, more than you know. Everything y'all did yesterday—that we all did yesterday—really changed the look of the trailer. It feels like home now, doesn't it?"

He nodded. "Mama would've liked it."

"She sees it," Rose said, "from heaven."

Oh, how Savvy loved these children. "I hope you all know how very blessed I am that your mom wanted me to take care of you," she said.

"We fixed breakfast for us, too, but it's on the table. We're gonna go eat it now, and then we can all get ready for church." Rose tugged on her sister's nightgown. "Come on, Daisy. Let's go eat cimminum toast."

"Okay," Daisy said, following her twin out of the room while Dylan remained behind.

"Are you going to eat cinnamon toast, too?" Savvy asked Dylan.

"Are you going to church with us?" he returned.

Savvy's stomach knotted as she recalled the last time she'd been at the Claremont Community Church. And everything she'd told Brodie last night pushed to the forefront of her thoughts. "I don't think so, Dylan." She wasn't ready, didn't know if she'd ever be ready. All of her heartache started at that church.

His eyes narrowed, shoulders dropped. "We made you breakfast because this is supposed to be a special day. But our mom is gone. And she wanted you to take care of us. And we want you to go to church. We don't want to go to church on Mother's Day and not have anyone there."

"Brodie will be there," Savvy said weakly.

Dylan shook his head and left the room while Savvy looked at the delicious food on her plate... and realized she'd completely lost her appetite.

Brodie arrived at the trailer at 9:00 a.m. the following morning to pick up the kids. He'd looked forward to being here again ever since he left last night, not only because he looked forward to taking the kids to church, but because he hoped that Savvy would come.

Their kiss had been pivotal, not only because it affirmed that she had feelings for him, too, but also because she hadn't allowed a man to kiss her in over a decade. And she'd trusted Brodie enough to let him be the first. So even though she hadn't said that she forgave him, he felt certain that she would, in time. And now that he knew her past, he understood why it took so long for her to build the ability to trust and the capacity to forgive.

Finding her faith again would put her on the road to spiritual healing, and Brodie had prayed throughout the morning that she'd start down that path today by going to church with him and the kids on Mother's Day. Dylan had expressed how much he wanted her to come today, not only because he wanted Savvy to attend church with them, but also because it was their first Mother's Day without their mom. He didn't want to be at the church without the woman who'd taken on the responsibility of caring for him and his sisters. And Brodie didn't want Dylan to be any more upset than he already was. He'd grown close to the teenager over the past few weeks, and he wanted to help him get through this difficult day. He pulled up and tapped his horn like every other time he picked the kids up for church. And like every other time, Rose and Daisy emerged first.

They wore similar floral dresses, Rose's pink and Daisy's yellow. Dylan, as usual, exited a moment after the twins and carried his Bible, as well as the girls' Bibles.

He yelled goodbye to Savvy at the door, and then closed it with an undeniable sadness darkening his features as he made his way to the truck. "I'll buckle them in," he said somberly, and he leaned into the extended cab to snap Rose's and Daisy's buckles into place.

Then he climbed into the front passenger seat.

Brodie stared at the door to the trailer.

"She isn't coming," Dylan said.

Disappointment flooding through him, Brodie nodded. He'd so hoped this would be the day Savvy would join them. Had prayed for it. But obviously, he'd asked for too much. "Okay, then," he said, putting the truck in Reverse.

"Oh, wait!" Daisy said, and Brodie slammed on his brakes.

"What is it?" he asked, turning toward the girls in the backseat.

"I forgot my—" She smiled as she looked toward the trailer. "Hey, Aunt Savvy got it for me."

Brodie turned to see Savvy, wearing a pale pink sundress and white sandals, exiting the trailer. She held Daisy's plant, the one with *MoMMy* painted on the side, in one hand and a Bible in the other. Her blond hair was pulled up with several curling wisps falling in front, and sparkling earrings dangled from her ears.

"I'll move to the backseat," Dylan said, hopping out of the front and then holding the door until Savvy climbed inside.

"Thank you, Dylan," she said.

"Thanks for getting Mommy's flower, Aunt Savvy," Daisy said.

"You're welcome," Savvy answered softly.

Dylan waited until Savvy buckled up, and then said, "Thank you, Aunt Savvy," before he closed her door and climbed into the backseat with the girls.

Brodie knew Dylan was grateful for her deciding to join them, probably nearly as grateful as Brodie was to God for answering his prayer.

Savvy gripped the tiny clay pot and the Bible as they drove to the church. She'd thought she wasn't ready for this, and she still wasn't sure that she was, but the look on Dylan's face when she'd told him she wasn't coming coupled with the idea that he and the girls and Brodie would be hurt if she didn't forced her to get up and get ready...and get in the truck.

Now, as Brodie joined in with the other cars lining up to enter the church parking area, Savvy's attention was drawn to the large expanse of land behind the church near the cemetery. She could almost see the red-and-white tent, almost hear the intoxicating voice of the man she'd loved. The one who, for a time, had stolen her heart... and her soul.

Savvy jumped when a hand touched her own, gripping that Bible like a lifeline.

"Hey," Brodie said, gently running his fingers over the top of her hand as he spoke. "We're here with you."

She nodded, and then she turned to the back-seat to see Rose and Daisy looking at her with smiles on their faces and undeniable love in their hearts. And then she pivoted a little more to see Dylan behind her, and he nodded, a simple gesture, but one that told Savvy he was glad she was here.

That vision, of the ones most important in her life now, sent a warm feeling of peace through her spirit. Or maybe it was the fact that she was here period, giving God another chance, that had her turn back around in the seat, look toward the church and only see the current picture. A beautiful spring day with a crowd gathering to worship. Families smiling and visiting as they crossed the parking lot to enter the building. Brother Henry waiting at the top step to greet everyone on this Mother's Day.

And then she saw the familiar white car that had shown up in their driveway last night, pulling in a few spaces down from the one where they'd parked. Savvy waited for the truck to stop, and then said to Brodie, "I'll be right back, okay?"

He grinned, apparently seeing the same thing that she'd seen and knowing where she was headed. "Okay."

She got out of the truck and walked toward her grandparents' car. Since her grandmother always took a little time to get her Bible, purse and anything else she needed, Jolaine Bowers still sat in the passenger's seat when Savvy opened her door.

She looked up in surprise, and then her mouth trembled, her eyes spilling over instantly with tears. "Oh, my. Oh, what a blessed day," she said.

"Happy Mother's Day," Savvy murmured.

"Oh, yes, dear. Yes, it is." She scrambled from the car to give Savvy a hug. "I'm so glad you're here." Then she glanced around. "Where's your family?"

Her family.

Savvy again fought back tears and pointed toward Brodie's truck. "They're right there," she said.

"Well, let's go see those kids. Did they sleep any after all of that cotton candy we fed them?" her grandfather asked.

Savvy laughed. "I thought it took them longer than usual to go to sleep."

"A little extra sugar every now and then never

hurt nobody," he declared, heading toward the truck, where Dylan was helping his sisters out. "Hey there, girls," he said.

"Hey, Pop Pop," Rose and Daisy returned, and Savvy's hand moved to her throat.

"Pop Pop?" Savvy whispered to her grand-mother.

"They wanted to know what to call him," Jolaine said, then gently punched an elbow in Savvy's side. "Watch this." She cleared her throat. "Hey, Rose. Hey, Daisy."

The twins beamed at her. "Hey, Mimi."

Savvy's heart overflowed. She couldn't imag-ine life getting much better. And then she looked up to the man who'd picked up the Bible and the tiny flowerpot she'd left on the seat. And her heart filled even more.

"You ready?" he asked.

She'd been ready for this her entire life. "Yes, I'm ready."

When the worship service ended, Savvy found that it took quite a while for them to exit their pew. Not because of the Mother's Day crowd, but because of how many members of that congrega-tion wanted to welcome her back. There were no whispers, no finger-pointings of accusation, no reminders of her past mistakes.

And Savvy began to feel the healing power of

forgiveness. Not her own inability to forgive, but the ability of all these people, several that she specifically remembered doing wrong at one time or another, welcoming her with open arms. Maybe it had something to do with Brother Henry's lesson. He'd spoken about Mother's Day, but then he'd transitioned to the power of forgiveness, and Savvy wondered if that part was primarily for her.

She'd been moved to tears, but she'd been careful that Dylan, Rose and Daisy didn't see her wipe them away. Brodie, however, must have noticed, because at the exact moment that she thought she couldn't breathe from the emotion filling her soul, he put his arm around her and pulled her closer to him on the pew. And Savvy found the strength to listen and believe every word.

Her heart welcomed the message, and so did her soul.

Brother Henry spoke about how Jesus had taught us to forgive. He also focused on the fact that not forgiving someone only hurts you, and Savvy couldn't help agreeing. She hadn't forgiven Tyler. That certainly hadn't hurt his life, but it had crippled her own.

She stood at the pew now and accepted one hug after another, and she realized many of these church members had helped her through the past few weeks, by sending the casseroles Mandy delivered or by offering prayers. Savvy was amazed at how much *I've been praying for you and the children* meant to her heart. She'd felt those prayers. Maybe she hadn't realized it at the time, but she'd had a growing peace since she arrived in Claremont, and now she suspected that her serenity had grown with each of those prayers.

One by one, people who used to look at Savvy with accusing eyes welcomed her into their fold. Then she saw Micca's family preparing to pass their pew. Savvy expected the principal to continue toward the exit, but Micca whispered something to her husband and then moved down the pew in front of Savvy until they stood face-to-face. Dylan had started talking to another boy his age, and Rose and Daisy chatted with a little girl who'd been in their Sunday school class while Brodie spoke to Mr. and Mrs. Tolleson, who'd been sitting on the pew behind them. So none of them seemed aware of the encounter Savvy feared was about to take place.

She held her breath.

Micca looked at Savvy's dress. "You look very pretty," she said, then added, "You always did."

Savvy noted Micca's outfit, a yellow dress with a crocheted jacket and pearls. Her makeup was more subdued today, and her hair had a few highlights that hadn't been there before. "You do, too," Savvy said. "I like your outfit."

Micca smiled. "My husband gave me a makeover for Mother's Day. I've always wanted one, but I never wanted to spend the money on myself." She self-consciously smoothed a wayward lock of hair back into place. "So I spent yesterday at the Cut and Curl, and then picked out the dress at the Consigning Women shop on the square. Maribeth Brooks owns it, and she selects the outfits based on things that celebrities wear."

"Really? I'll have to check it out," Savvy replied. She'd seen the shop on the other side of the square from the sporting-goods store, but she hadn't had an opportunity to go inside yet.

"I like it," Micca said.

Savvy could tell the lady, who'd held no kind words for Savvy during their meeting at the school, was having a tough time saying whatever she wanted to say. But Savvy knew what she wanted to say to Micca. "I know I said this before, but please let me reiterate how very sorry I am for how I was in high school and for the way I treated you. It was wrong. I was wrong. And I hate it that I hurt you. I know that you may not be ready to yet, but I hope that one day you'll forgive me."

Micca bit her lower lip, then glanced at Rose and Daisy, who were still chatting with the little girl from class. "I can tell that you've changed, Savvy. And I do believe that you're truly sorry." She smiled a little toward the girls, even though

Rose and Daisy weren't paying attention to their principal at the moment. "And that sermon this morning reminded me that I've hurt myself more than anyone else with the animosity that I've held toward you over the years. So I do forgive you, Savvy."

Savvy leaned forward and hugged her. She could tell by the way Micca's entire body bristled that she wasn't expecting it, or maybe she wasn't all that used to being hugged by someone she'd hated a week ago, but that was what Savvy wanted to do, so she did. And eventually, Micca's tension eased, and she chuckled.

"Okay, then, that's probably good," she said.

Savvy released her. "I'm sorry. It's just that I'm very, very grateful for your forgiveness."

"Well, then," Micca said, "you're welcome." She smiled at her husband, who'd left the auditorium but stepped back inside to motion for her to come on. Then she exited the pew, and Savvy turned to see that Mr. and Mrs. Tolleson had also left, and Brodie had observed the tail end of their conversation.

"That's pretty awesome, huh?" he murmured.

"Yes," she agreed. "It is."

"Can we take Mommy's flower now?" Daisy asked.

"Sure," Savvy said, and they joined in with the others exiting the auditorium.

Brother Henry, as usual, stood at the door leading outside. When he saw them approaching, he nodded at Savvy. "This is indeed a blessed day," he said. He shook Brodie's hand and then said to the kids, "Did y'all enjoy the lesson?"

"I like the part where we get to come down front the best," Rose said.

"That's one of my favorite parts, too," Brother Henry confided to her and Daisy.

Dylan held out his hand. "I enjoyed the lesson, Brother Henry," he said with a maturity that went beyond his thirteen years. Savvy supposed that he'd matured even more over the past few weeks, losing his mother and then learning to cope with his new life. Savvy could relate to that, and she admired the young man he was becoming, and the fact that Brodie was already such an integral part of his life.

"I'm glad you did, son," Brother Henry said, smiling at Dylan.

The kids continued down the stairs, and Brother Henry focused on Savvy. "What did *you* think of the lesson?" he asked candidly.

"Like it was meant just for me," she answered, "though I'm sure others benefited from it, also. But I needed it," she said. "So much."

He nodded, took her hand and squeezed it. "I thought you might. And I want you to know that

I'm here if you need to talk. It was truly a blessing seeing you in church today."

"Thank you, Brother Henry," Savvy said. "I'll be back."

"I'm counting on it," he replied, then turned to the next family exiting the auditorium while Brodie and Savvy joined Dylan, Rose and Daisy at the foot of the stairs.

Daisy cradled the tiny flowerpot in her hands, and she looked toward the cemetery. "Can we go take this to where Mommy is?"

Savvy nodded. "Sure, honey."

"I'm going to wait by the truck," Dylan said.

"You don't want to go see where Mommy is?" Rose asked.

"She isn't there," Dylan said.

Savvy wanted to make sure she handled this correctly, since Rose and Daisy had both turned to see how she'd respond. "You're right, Dylan," she said. "Your mom is in heaven, and she's having a wonderful time there, I'm sure."

"But what about her flower?" Daisy asked, a hint of panic in her tone. "How do we let her see her flower?"

"We can still put her flower there," Brodie reassured her, "and it will make her happy knowing that you planted it for her and put it by her name."

Savvy was glad he didn't say anything about a tombstone, or grave, or anything else that sounded morbid. "Putting it by her name" was perfect. *Thank you,* she mouthed to him, and he nodded.

"Rose, Daisy," Brodie said, "I'll help you find the spot where we can put your flower for your mommy. Brother Henry told me exactly where to find it. You can stay here, if you like," he said to Savvy, apparently knowing that she felt the need to talk to Dylan.

The girls followed Brodie toward the small church cemetery behind the building, and Savvy stayed with Dylan.

He made no effort to go to the truck, but stared after Brodie and his sisters as they entered the cemetery. "She isn't there," he repeated.

"I know," Savvy said gently.

"Do you think..." he started, then flexed his jaw as though forcing himself to hold it together. "Do you think she can see us? Do you think she knows I'm sorry?"

Savvy prayed she'd get this right, and the sense of peace that washed over her told her God was listening and helping. "I'm not sure what heaven is like, what you see or hear, but I know that your mom knows that you love her, and I know that she wouldn't think there was anything for you to apologize for." She reached out and gently squeezed his shoulder. "She's in heaven, Dylan. So she's happy. No more pain. No more worries. And she knew when she died that I would take care of all of you."

He slung his hair away, and she saw the concern in those somber blue eyes. "You're glad for that? That she picked you, and that you're here?"

Savvy hadn't anticipated part of his sadness came from doubting her desire to be here. She'd thought she'd made it clear to the kids how she felt. But she didn't want him having any doubt.

"I love you, Dylan. And I love Rose and Daisy. Your mom must've known that I would, because she'd have wanted you to be loved. And I feel so very blessed that she trusted me to raise all of you." Her voice quivered with emotion. "Because I've never had a family like this, and you and your sisters *are* my family now. I will thank your mama every day for giving me this blessing."

His mouth crept up on both sides, showcasing those deep dimples. "That's good," he said. "'Cause I guess you're stuck with us now, huh?"

"Can't imagine anything I'd rather be," Savvy said, and then she stepped toward him and hugged him. She wasn't certain whether he'd pull away, maybe being too cool for a hug, but he didn't. He allowed her this sweet luxury, and then he slowly backed away.

"Thanks, Aunt Savvy," he said quietly as Brodie and the girls returned.

"You're welcome."

"I thought you were going to the truck," Rose said.

Dylan grinned. "We are. Come on, and I'll help buckle y'all in."

They ran ahead, while Savvy felt Brodie move beside her, his hand naturally capturing hers and clasping it as they walked across the parking lot.

"They were happy about putting the flower on her grave," he said. "How's Dylan?"

"He's good. Just wondering about heaven, and whether his mom can see him now."

"Big questions," he said.

"Yeah, and I'm glad he felt comfortable asking me."

"You're a great mom already," Brodie said as they neared the truck.

Savvy's heart swelled with gratitude. "Thanks."

"Brodie! Savvy!" her grandmother yelled at them from her car window as she and Savvy's grandfather started across the parking lot.

"What's up?" Savvy asked.

"I meant to ask you last night when we brought the kids home, but we are grilling out at the fishing hole today and would love for y'all to come. The kids can swim if they want. Just swing by your place and get their suits. Sound good?"

"Sounds great to me," she said. "You in, Brodie?"

"Yeah," he said, smiling at Savvy. "I'm all in."

Chapter Thirteen

Brodie parked the truck at the trailer and laughed at the snoring princesses in the backseat. "Swimming wore them out," he said to Savvy.

He watched her turn in the seat to peek at Rose and Daisy, leaning against each other and clutching the stuffed teddy bears Savvy's grandmother had given them this afternoon. Jolaine gave teddy bears to all of the younger grandchildren, and beach balls to the older ones.

Brodie had been incredibly touched by the entire afternoon, not only that Savvy's grandparents had welcomed the kids—and him—to their family gathering, but also that the kids had joined in without hesitation. Dylan spent his time fishing with Savvy's teenage cousins—Troy Lee's younger brothers—and the twins swam and played with Savvy's cousin Becca's five-year-old daughter, Lily.

"You want me to carry one of them in?" Dylan asked Brodie.

"Sure," he said.

Dylan scooped up Daisy and headed for the trailer, and Brodie followed with Rose while Savvy gathered the bags of wet swimsuits and beach towels. She followed Dylan and Brodie to the girls' room.

"We'll just leave their T-shirts and shorts on to sleep in tonight," she whispered. "I don't want to wake them."

Dylan and Brodie nodded, slid the girls beneath the covers and then they all left the bedroom, while Rose and Daisy never broke stride in their snoring.

"Okay if I watch TV until it's time to go to bed?" Dylan asked.

Savvy nodded. "Sure, and thanks for helping us bring the girls in."

"No problem." He sat on the couch in the living room, and as Brodie and Savvy started outside, he said, "Hey, Coach?"

Brodie stopped, his hand on the door. "Yeah?"

"There's a baseball thing after school on Tuesday for the junior high kids, a one-day camp with the high school guys teaching and stuff. I was thinking I might go to it, you know." He'd been looking at his hands when he spoke, but then he chanced a glance at Brodie, apparently to gauge his thoughts on the subject. "You think I'd do okay at it?"

Savvy's quick intake of breath said his question surprised her as much as Brodie. Dylan wanted so much to be on the team, and letting the coach—as well as the high school players—see what he could do was undeniably a great first step at making that happen. But he hadn't had the confidence before. Now he did, and Brodie felt truly blessed at having a part in that. "You'll do great," he assured him.

Dylan grinned. "Aunt Savvy, I'll be staying after school on Tuesday for that, okay?"

She blinked a couple of times and then nodded. "Sure."

"Cool," Dylan said, and then picked up the remote and changed the channel.

"Night, buddy," Brodie murmured, smiling at Savvy before leading the way outside.

He'd barely closed the door when she whispered, "What about that? Isn't it wonderful that he's putting himself out there?"

Brodie grinned. "Very wonderful," he said. "And he's going to surprise those guys. He's very good."

"Thanks to you," she insisted.

"Well, I like to think I've helped, but he's got natural talent. He just needed a little training, that's all."

They found their respective seats on the deck steps. "We should probably buy you a swing or something," he said, "some other place for us to sit and talk in the evening besides these wooden steps. They're not the most comfortable of seating options."

She grinned. "Hey, I like these steps. They aren't warped anymore, and even if a rain comes, we can sit out here now without getting wet, thanks to that new awning." She nudged her shoulder into his side. "Don't knock my steps."

He laughed. "I guess I shouldn't, since I helped build them."

"Exactly."

His phone rang, and he pulled it from his pocket and checked the display. "It's a Knoxville number, but it isn't Cherie's."

"Maybe it's Marissa," she said. "I'll go inside so you can talk to her in private."

She started to stand, but Brodie placed his hand on hers and shook his head. "No, stay." So she scooted closer to him, and Brodie kissed her cheek, then answered the phone. "Hello."

"Hey," she said quietly. "Um, it's Marissa."

Brodie had prayed she'd call, but now that she did, he wasn't sure what to say. "Hey," he began, and then asked, "Everything okay?"

"Yeah," she said, and then the line grew quiet again.

Savvy's eyebrows lifted in a silent question about what was happening.

Brodie shrugged, unsure. "I'm glad you called," he said.

"I, well, we all went to church today. The preacher talked about Mother's Day mostly, but then he talked about forgiveness."

Brodie nodded. "That sounds like the lesson I heard this morning, too."

"You went to church today?" she asked, obviously a little surprised at this revelation.

Brodie didn't mind that she'd assumed he wouldn't go. Until her accident, he hadn't. "I did, and it was a great lesson."

"Ours was, too," she said softly. "And when the preacher was talking about it, I thought about how you said you were sorry, you know, for not staying with me and Mom."

"I am sorry," Brodie reiterated. "I can't even express how much I'm sorry."

"I love my dad," she said quickly.

Brodie's heart fisted in his chest. He wasn't the man she thought of as "Dad," but maybe he could still be something. "I know you do."

"Yeah, um, I talked to him and Mom today and told them that I thought I should probably do what the preacher says. I'm supposed to forgive, but it's hard, you know?"

"I do know," he said thickly.

"But I could've died in that accident. The doctors said so, and everybody else said the same thing. And if I did, then I wouldn't have ever, you know, got to at least meet you or anything. And even though I have a dad, you— Well, you were my dad first."

Brodie blinked through the impact of her words. Just to hear her call him Dad, in any sense of the word, sent arrows of awareness to his heart. He had a daughter. He'd left that daughter. But he desperately wanted her back in his life.

"Dad said that if I want to, you know, let you visit or something, then I can. And Mom said it was up to me, too."

Brodie couldn't stop the hope that soared through him with her words. "Is that something you want?"

Another pause echoed through the line, and then she said, "I think so."

"That'd mean..." he started, then swallowed. "That'd mean a lot to me. You just let me know when, and I'm there. Or you can come here. Or we can meet somewhere in the middle," he said, his excitement causing him to speak faster with every word.

Her soft laugh echoed through the line. "Okay."

Brodie really liked hearing her laugh; he hoped to hear it again often. And he wanted to stay on the phone with her, get a glimpse of her life. "So did you have a nice Mother's Day with your mom?"

"Yeah. We went to church and out to eat. Then

we played board games tonight. That's what Mom likes to do, so we wanted to do what she wanted."

"That sounds like a good day," he said. Cherie had always enjoyed staying in and spending time together during the brief time they dated and when they married, but Brodie hadn't appreciated that type of simplicity before. Now, with Savvy by his side, he understood the value of time spent together, and he hoped to always spend plenty of quality time with Savvy and the kids like today, for Mother's Day.

Which made Brodie realize what he hadn't thought to do today. "Marissa, is your mom nearby?"

"In the next room," she said.

"When you get a chance, would you tell her happy Mother's Day for me?"

A pause echoed through the line, but then Marissa softly said, "Sure, I'll tell her." She waited another beat. "We'll talk again soon, I guess?"

Brodie blinked, awestruck at the fact that he would be talking to her on a regular basis. "Yes, soon." Then she said goodbye and disconnected.

Savvy, obviously listening to every word from his end of the conversation, leaned toward him. "Brodie, did Marissa forgive you?"

He still held the phone and looked at it, almost disbelieving that the conversation had transpired. "Yes, she did, and I think this is a sign that Cherie is getting there, as well." He sighed. "After all these years, I'm finally going to have a place in my daughter's life."

"You'll be a terrific father," she said.

"She has a father already," he said. "Ryan. He's been her daddy all this time. I guess that's what makes this so incredible, because it was Ryan's idea to call me that night from the hospital." He shook his head. "I can't get over how amazing it felt to hear Marissa say she forgives me. God is definitely answering my prayers. It was just like Brother Henry said this morning—true forgiveness holds no limitations."

Brodie looked to Savvy, hoping that perhaps she might find it in her heart to forgive him, too. But instead of saying those words he wanted to hear, she cleared her throat, opened her mouth… and then closed it without speaking.

Chapter Fourteen

Savvy spent the day inventorying the stockroom, not because that'd been on the schedule of things to do, but because it kept her in the back of the store on her own, instead of up front with her grandparents. They'd been so excited when she arrived this morning, talking about how wonderful it was to have her at church and with the family at the fishing hole, as well as how much they adored Brodie and the kids. You could almost hear wedding bells when her grandmother spoke of Savvy and Brodie.

But Brodie expected her to forgive him; she had heard it in his voice last night when he talked about Cherie and Marissa forgiving him, and she'd seen the expectant look on his face as he waited for Savvy to say she forgave him, too. But as she was about to speak the words, something held her back.

Was it the memory of Willow's voice cracking when she'd finally told Savvy about the way Brodie had left her in that hotel room? Or knowing that Willow had only been with Brodie because she'd assumed they were in love, and then he abandoned her? Savvy knew all too well how it felt to be abandoned by someone who supposedly loved you, first from her mother and then from Ty.

And even last night, in spite of how close she and Brodie had become, she still remembered what he'd done to Willow. How could she tell him she forgave him if she couldn't forget? Would she never be able to, and would she always feel lousy about it, the way she felt now?

Savvy dropped a heavy box of tennis rackets on the floor with a loud bang, which caused her grandmother to dash into the stockroom.

"Everything okay?" she asked, glancing around the room to find the source of the noise.

Savvy grunted as she lifted the box to a nearby table. "Everything's fine."

"What's wrong, honey?" her grandmother asked.

Savvy easily slipped into the ways of her past, specifically high school, when she had so often lied to her grandmother without batting an eye. "I'm worried about the kids," she said. "They're all taking the standardized achievement tests today, and whether they're promoted to the next grade depends on how they score." It wasn't exactly a lie, because she was concerned about the kids' test scores, but that wasn't what was wrong.

So maybe it was a lie.

"Oh, honey, we've been praying for them nonstop, and you told me yesterday that you think they're ready, right? Brodie said the same thing."

Savvy jabbed a racket into a slot on the shelf. "Right."

"Why don't you take a walk on the square and get some fresh air? Maybe go down to the Sweet Stop and pick up a lemon square. Those always cheer me up."

Savvy didn't have the heart to tell her that nothing could fix what bothered her, not even a sugary lemon square. So instead of trying to explain, she conceded, "You're right. I'm going to take a walk and maybe get something from the Sweet Stop."

"Good deal." Jolaine put her arm around Savvy and gently patted her shoulder. "I'll hold down the fort here while you're gone. No worries."

"Thanks," Savvy said, her stomach feeling sick that she was undeniably lying again.

She stepped out the front door and had to blink to adjust to the scene. A gentle breeze pushed through the oak trees that bordered the three-tiered fountain centering the square, causing the leaves to sway. The fountain water splashed and sparkled like wet diamonds in the brilliant sunlight. Several elderly couples sat on wrought iron benches feeding squawking geese. Shoppers visited, smiling and chatting, as they passed each other on the sidewalk.

The beauty of the May afternoon on the square seemed wrong. Savvy felt miserable, and it made no sense that everything around her looked perfectly fine.

She glanced up to see Mandy and Daniel Brantley heading toward her on the sidewalk with their baby, Mia, perched on her mom's hip. "Hey, Savvy," Mandy said, her voice as cheerful as ever. "We're heading to Nelson's for a late lunch. Wanna join us?"

"No," she said, "but thanks."

"Okay," Mandy said, smiling down at Mia as she withdrew her dark hair from the baby's fist. Savvy was glad that she seemed more focused on Mia than Savvy's sour mood. Then Mandy looked to Savvy, and her head tilted as though she might actually know how Savvy felt.

Savvy forced a smile.

"You know, Kaden has been talking about how much fun he had with the girls on those couple of days we came out to your place," Mandy said. "Why don't you let us pick them up after school tomorrow and take them to Hydrangea Park to play? That'd give you a little time to relax."

Savvy could explain that relaxing wasn't her current problem, but that would prompt an actual heart-to-heart discussion, and she certainly wasn't ready to do that. So she forced another smile and said, "Sure, that'd be great."

"Wonderful. I'll get them when I pick up Kaden. You'll just need to send a note with them to school that it's okay for me to pick them up."

Savvy nodded. "I will." Then they said goodbye and continued their trek toward Nelson's while she started toward the Sweet Stop, since that was what she'd told her grandmother she'd do. She'd already lied to her *twice*; she wouldn't lie to her about going to the candy shop, too.

But she'd only traveled a short distance down the sidewalk when she crossed paths with someone who looked as miserable as Savvy felt. And the lady stopped in her tracks when she saw Savvy.

Savvy took a deep breath and didn't know if she was ready to face Willow's mother. But since the woman had already started toward her with an accusing finger pointed at Savvy's face, she didn't see how she had a choice.

"You," Lorina said, her voice shaking with hatred.

This wasn't the day to pick a fight with Savvy, and she had no reason at all to pretend to be happy for Lorina Jackson's sake.

"What have I ever done to you?" Savvy asked. "If anyone has the right to be mad here, it's me. Whether you were the one who abused Willow in your home or not—and I honestly think it was your husband—you still didn't stop him. How do you sleep at night?"

A thick vein pulsed in Lorina's forehead, reminding Savvy of her husband on the day he had tried to attack Brodie.

"Frank wouldn't have been so angry with her all the time if she'd have done what he said and stayed away from you and Brodie Evans. Always getting into trouble, you three. Nothing but trouble."

"You're blaming *us* for what happened inside your home?" Savvy asked in disbelief.

"Well, what do you expect? She acted so foolish because of you, and her daddy and I warned her we wouldn't come help if she threw her life away. And that's exactly what she did." She scowled at Savvy. "And when it all hit the wall and she got pregnant, where were her precious friends then? You were gone…and so was he."

Savvy's skin burned, partly because of the accusation and partly because Lorina was right. Savvy *hadn't* been there for Willow when she'd needed her most. "That's something I'll have to live with the rest of my life," Savvy said. "But I'm here for her now. I'm doing what she wanted, taking care of her children. And I love them. I do."

"What about *him*? Frank said he saw the two of you together, you and that Evans boy. Said he thought you two looked like you were an item now." She shook her head. "He has no limits to how low he'll stoop. *Now* he's going to come around and pretend he's some kind of good guy with those kids? Now? After Wendy's gone? If he had been there for her in the beginning, she'd never have gotten pregnant again with those girls."

Savvy balled her fists to keep from hitting the woman. "*Those girls* are your granddaughters, and they're precious!"

A few people had started toward them on the sidewalk but, seeing the two of them yelling and red faced, turned the other direction.

"The girls are just like her boy. The first time, Wendy got herself pregnant by a no-account, good-for-nothing guy who only wanted one thing and then left after he got it. The second time, same thing. Their father didn't support them or Wendy either, now, did he?"

"Their father was going to marry Willow, but he died before the wedding." Savvy pushed the words through her clenched jaw.

"So she said," Lorina hissed. "He was no better than Brodie."

"Brodie?" Why was she comparing the girls' father to Brodie?

"I'm telling you that if Brodie Evans had done the right thing to begin with, then Wendy would have had the opportunity to be something. But he didn't. He was making it big playing baseball, and Frank told me those guys make plenty. But he never even sent her anything to help her out. Never cared about supporting his own child!"

Savvy had already drawn a breath to continue her verbal battle, but those last two words hit her with a one-two punch that offered no recovery. *His own child.* "Wh-what?"

Lorina's penciled eyebrows rose with a violent jerk, and for the first time ever, Savvy watched the lady smile. Or rather, sneer. "You didn't know." Then she laughed, an evil, wet sound. "I didn't, either. I mean, who knew who she was sleeping with back then?"

"*Don't* talk about her that way," Savvy warned, still reeling from what Lorina insinuated.

The older woman shrugged her bony shoulders and went on, "She'd never told me either until a couple of months ago, when I saw her right here on the square. That was the first time I'd seen her in years, because she never had money to do anything." She pursed her lips. "She was too embarrassed to be seen in town. She was shopping for those kids, and I told her if she'd have had even one guy who did the right thing by her, maybe she wouldn't be scraping by with nothing." She shook her head in disgust again. "That's when she said that Dylan's father, Brodie Evans, would be a part of her life soon."

Savvy's hand moved to her chest, and the scene that had looked so beautiful a moment ago swirled into a hideous mass of colors that refused to blend.

Lorina continued staring at Savvy with that sinister smile. "Looks like you and your new boyfriend have a few things to discuss," she said, and then she turned and left Savvy standing on the sidewalk, her world spinning bizarrely out of control.

"Savvy, dear, are you okay?" Her grandmother rushed to her side. "Diane Marsh called me from her store, said she saw Lorina Jackson yelling at you. What was going on? Was it about Willow? Or the kids? Is she angry Willow left them to you? I thought they didn't want anything to do with their grandchildren."

"They don't," Savvy said dully.

"Then what did she want?"

Savvy couldn't talk about it. She barely comprehended it. "I need to go home," she said numbly.

"Of course, dear. That's fine. Take the rest of the day. Take the rest of the week if you want."

Savvy nodded, then started toward her truck

so she could head home to wait for the children. Rose, Daisy…and Brodie's son.

She drove to the trailer without paying attention to anything beyond her thoughts. Why hadn't she considered the possibility that Brodie was Dylan's father?

Savvy tried to remember the letter she'd read that first day when Brodie showed up at the trailer, the last letter Willow had written before she died. She didn't recall anything that would've indicated he was Dylan's father, but that had been the last thing on her mind back then. She needed to see that letter again, and she'd rather see it before she saw Brodie. Yet deep down inside, she knew, even without seeing the letter. Brodie was Dylan's dad. So many things clicked into place now. The love of baseball and natural talent that even Brodie recognized. The problem with math and reading comprehension, subjects Brodie also struggled in. The dark hair. Those blue eyes. The dimples.

Why hadn't Savvy seen it? And why hadn't Brodie considered it, either?

Brodie had no idea that the boy he'd grown so close to over the past month was his son.

Savvy would have to tell him, and soon. She couldn't imagine how he'd feel, how Dylan would feel, when they realized the truth.

She drove down the driveway leading to the

trailer, and her heart thudded in her chest when she saw the big black truck parked in its regular spot, and Brodie sitting on the tailgate. Several shiny, multicolored balloons hovered a few feet above his head with the captions "Good Job!", "Proud of You!" and "Way to Go!" stamped on each.

He lifted a hand and gave her a smile as she parked, and Savvy's pulse raced. Maybe he wasn't upset with her for not being able to say she forgave him, and now Savvy wondered why it seemed so hard. She'd been upset with him for what he had done to Willow, but Willow had forgiven him, clearly, or she wouldn't have written that letter and planned to tell him the truth. If her friend could stop blaming him, then surely Savvy could, as well. That didn't mean that she'd forget what he'd done, but undoubtedly Willow had never forgotten what happened that night, yet she'd been ready to give him a place in Dylan's life. *That* was the type of forgiveness Brother Henry had talked about yesterday, and that was the type of forgiveness Savvy wanted—needed—to give Brodie.

Maybe she'd felt as if she would be betraying Willow's memory if she forgave the man who hurt her, but now that she knew how completely Willow had forgiven Brodie, she also knew that Willow wouldn't have wanted Savvy to hold that mistake over his head forever. She'd have wanted

Savvy to forgive. And Savvy knew that was why she'd felt so terrible today, because she hadn't said what she needed to say, hadn't done what she needed to do last night.

She'd change that soon. First she'd tell him what she'd learned from Lorina, and then she'd tell him that she forgave him. Savvy grinned, realizing she was probably about to give him the best news of his life, that Dylan was his son. And then she thought of what it could mean for her and Brodie. Maybe the two of them could look at this as something God had planned, for them to raise Dylan, Rose and Daisy together as a family.

A surge of excitement rushed through Savvy. She parked the truck and hopped out, hurried toward the handsome coach sitting on the bed of his truck.

"For test day," he said, grinning as he pointed to the balloons, which Savvy now noticed were each tied to a king-size candy bar. "They should be getting off the bus any minute, and I wanted to be here, to let them know we're proud, no matter what."

"That's great! Brodie, you're—" she began, and then changed her mind about saying that he was Dylan's father. That wasn't the type of thing you simply blurted out. Plus, she wanted to somehow make Willow a part of the announcement, and she thought she might have a way of doing it. "That letter Willow mailed to you, when she was asking you to help Dylan..."

He nodded. "I keep it in my wallet now."

Savvy hadn't thought of that. She really wanted to see that letter, find out if it held a hint toward Dylan being his son, and show it to him. That way, Willow would still tell him about Dylan, the way she'd wanted right before she died. "Can I read it again?" she asked.

He nodded, pulled his wallet out of his pocket and withdrew the folded letter. "Sure. I plan to keep it with me forever, because that's what brought me here." He smiled again, and Savvy couldn't wait to read it, show him the tiny clues they'd missed and let him put two and two together, with Willow's help.

Savvy took the precious piece of paper, unfolded it and began to read. Yes, she'd read it before, but not like this, focusing on every word, looking for clues, hints, anything that would say Willow planned to tell Brodie about Dylan.

The bus brakes screeched. "Hey, the kids are coming," he said.

Savvy frantically scanned the letter again, saw where Willow asked him to work with Dylan on schoolwork, but found nothing about Willow needing to talk to Brodie beyond that, or anything that would indicate Dylan was his son.

"Mr. Brodie!" Rose called, running up the driveway with Daisy at her heels. "Are those for us?"

Brodie grabbed two of the balloons, handed one to Rose and one to Daisy. "Yep, for taking those tests today."

"Mine says Good Job!" Rose said. "And I got a chocolate bar, too."

"Mine says Way to Go!" Daisy told her sister, then asked Savvy, "Can we eat our chocolate now?"

"Sure," she replied as the girls ran to the trailer. And then, still holding the letter, she watched the driveway for Dylan.

Finally emerging, he grinned as he walked toward them. And Savvy realized, now that she knew the truth, even the way he walked reminded her of his dad.

"I'm pretty sure I aced those tests," he said. "The reading was way easier when I watched for things I'd need to know."

"Told you," Brodie said, grinning back as he held the last balloon and chocolate combination toward Dylan.

Dylan raised his eyebrows. "I'm a little old for balloons, don't you think?"

"You saying you don't want it?" Brodie asked.

"I didn't say that." Dylan took the balloons and candy.

Savvy watched the two of them interacting,

wondered whether she should tell them together, and then decided she should tell Brodie first, and let *him* tell his son. She waited until Dylan entered the trailer. Then she looked back down at Willow's letter.

And saw the date at the top.

"Brodie, this is dated March seventh," she said. "But you didn't get it until the week she died?"

His smile slid into a frown as his eyes zeroed in on that date at the top of the letter. "No," he said. "I got it in early March."

"But…" Savvy remembered when he'd showed up with that letter, the day after she got the kids. Five days after Willow died. In April. "You didn't come until—" she calculated the days "—nearly a month later?"

He exhaled thickly, slowly reached for the letter and took it from Savvy. "I got this before Marissa's accident. And I was a different person then. I didn't think about the letter as a chance to help Dylan, not then. I could only think that if I responded to it, I'd see Willow. I knew how I'd treated her the last time I saw her, and I didn't want to—"

Savvy couldn't believe what he was saying. "You didn't want to see her? You didn't want to have a chance to say you were sorry for sleeping with her and then leaving her alone in a hotel room?" Savvy tried to wrap her mind around the fact that Brodie had had that letter for *weeks* before he'd come to see Willow. "If you'd come after you got it, you'd have seen her before she died. She'd have told you…"

She couldn't finish the sentence. Her mind spun with the possibilities of things that could've been if he hadn't ignored that letter. Willow would've told him about Dylan. He'd have learned he had a son. They might have rekindled those old feelings they'd found back then. Willow wouldn't have needed to take Dylan on that camping trip to tell him about his dad, because he'd have *had* his dad!

And the most prominent fact of all: if Brodie had come then, Willow might still be alive.

"How—how could you have ignored it?" Savvy asked, every muscle in her body tense from trying to keep her emotions together enough to speak. "*Why* did you?"

"I shouldn't have, Savvy. And I regret that more than I can say," he said, reaching for her.

She shook his arm off, stepped away from the truck. "No, you don't, or you would've told me. You wouldn't have acted as if you'd just gotten that letter when you showed up that day. You would've admitted that you'd put Willow's request for you to help Dylan on hold. Until she died!" Savvy couldn't control her raised voice, or her fury toward this man who could've saved her friend.

She'd nearly told him he was Dylan's father. But Brodie had treated Willow terribly fifteen years ago…and he'd treated her terribly again, disregarding her request as though it didn't matter, as though she didn't matter. Savvy had planned to tell him today that she forgave him for what he'd done back then, but he didn't deserve forgiveness. And he had *no* right to be Dylan's father now. Not after everything he'd put the boy's mother through.

But what if, merely because they shared blood, Brodie decided he wanted to raise his son himself? What if he took Dylan away from Savvy? Savvy loved Dylan, Rose and Daisy. They were her family now, and she couldn't imagine her life without them. She wouldn't let Brodie have the chance to take Dylan and then hurt and disappoint him in the same way he'd hurt and disappointed his mother time and again.

"You lied," she said.

"I didn't, Savvy. I never lied about it."

She bristled with anger. "You didn't tell me the truth about this letter. You let me believe you came as soon as you got it, and that you wanted to see Willow and help Dylan."

"I *did* want to see her. I *did* want to help Dylan."

"*After* you realized that was the only way to have a relationship with Marissa, *not* because you wanted to do the right thing by Willow." She had to get away from him before she blurted the truth. She would keep that secret to herself, because she didn't want Brodie around anymore, not when he had such a capacity to hurt. Dylan didn't need that.

And neither did Savvy.

"I'm glad that you've helped Dylan get ready for the test. And I think it's good that you helped him with baseball, too," she said, continuing to back away from the truck and move toward the trailer. Needing distance between her and this man. Because even now, when she was so mad she could hardly speak, she wanted to be comforted...by him.

What was wrong with her?

"But your job is done now," she went on. "He took the test today, and he'll have a school coach for baseball. We—we don't need you here anymore."

"Savvy, those aren't the only reasons I come here, and you know it. I love Dylan, and Rose and Daisy. But I don't just come here to see them. I thought you and I—"

"You thought wrong," she snapped, not even wanting to hear him say anything about the two of them together. That dream was over, like every other dream in Savvy's life. "I can't be with someone who would treat Willow that way and treat me this way."

And she wasn't going to let Dylan be hurt by a father who'd treat *him* this way, either. Dylan, Rose and Daisy had endured enough pain for a lifetime; Savvy was going to make certain they didn't suffer any more. And Brodie had proved, not only in the past, but again today, that he couldn't be trusted.

"You want me to leave?" he asked, shaking his head in disbelief.

"I do."

"I don't believe you, Savvy." He moved toward her, put his arm around her and tried to pull her close.

"Believe me, Brodie," she said, torn. All she wanted was to stay in his arms, have him hold her, tell him that the two of them could raise the kids together. Tell him that he was Dylan's father, and that he could be a father to Rose and Daisy, too. But he'd fooled her, in the same way Ty had fooled her before. And she wouldn't let him deceive those precious children into believing he would always be there for them when she knew he wouldn't. "Goodbye, Brodie," she said, pulling free and then hurrying away to enter the trailer.

She'd barely closed the door when Dylan's words assaulted her. "You told him not to come back," he said. "I heard you."

Thankfully, Rose and Daisy had gone to their room to play, and Savvy said a quick prayer that they wouldn't hear this interaction, because she had no idea how much their brother had heard. "Dylan, you've finished the tests now, and you're ready to work out with the high school baseball team. So you don't need Brodie's help anymore," she said, her emotions churning out of control.

He narrowed his eyes at her, but Savvy had been around him enough that she realized he wasn't angry. He was hurt. Which stabbed a dagger through her heart. She never wanted these kids to hurt again, but there was nothing she could do about this pain, especially when she realized that, without the television on to drown out the conversation outside, Dylan had been privy to every word.

"Is it true?" he asked.

She swallowed, dreading whatever he would ask. "Is what true?"

"He got that letter a month before he came?"

Savvy wanted to lie, but she knew it would only hurt Dylan more. And he'd already heard the answer. So she simply nodded, tears sliding down her cheeks. "I'm sorry," she whispered.

Dylan's jaw flexed, the same way Brodie's flexed when he fought emotions. And then he shook his head, stormed to his room and slammed the door.

Chapter Fifteen

Savvy hadn't slept. And it took everything she had to get the kids ready for school. Dylan hadn't come out of his room for breakfast and hadn't spoken when he'd left with the girls to catch the bus.

Savvy didn't know what to say to him, so she didn't try. Which made her feel like a complete failure. She needed help, and she thought she knew where to find it. So after the kids were gone, she called her grandmother.

"Hey, Savvy," she answered on the first ring. "Everything okay?"

Savvy worked hard at making her voice sound normal. "Yes, but I need to talk to someone today. And I was wondering if I could take you up on having today off."

"Sure, dear. Take as much time as you need," she said. "Your granddaddy and I will be praying for you."

Savvy closed her eyes. She desperately needed those prayers, so she'd take them. "Thanks."

Throughout the night, through all of the tears over telling Brodie to leave and seeing Dylan so upset, she'd also found herself praying. And she'd known that she couldn't live with herself withholding the truth from Brodie. But she also didn't know if she could live with herself if she told him the truth and he ended up hurting Dylan.

She found her Bible, opened it and withdrew the church bulletin she'd tucked inside Sunday morning. Then she dialed the number at the top of the page.

"Claremont Community Church," a sweet elderly voice answered.

"Hello," Savvy said. "Is Brother Henry there?"

"No, he isn't, dear," the woman said. "But this is his wife, Mary. Would I be able to help you?"

Savvy had so hoped to talk to him this morning. "I really just needed to speak with him," she said.

"He's at the hospital for Sister Sorrell's surgery. But he should be back around one. Would you like to come see him then?"

"Yes, please," Savvy said, grateful that the kids were all taken care of this afternoon so she'd be able to spend some much-needed time with the preacher.

"And may I tell him who this is?" Mary continued.

"I'm sorry. This is Savvy. Savvy Bowers."

"Savvy." Mary's voice grew even more tender. "I know he'll be happy to talk to you, dear."

"Thank you," Savvy said, then hung up and looked at the clock. Five hours until one. Five hours had never seemed so long.

Brodie had what he had initially wanted—a place in his daughter's life. But he was anything but happy. Anything but satisfied. Because over the past couple of months, he'd grown to love Dylan and Rose and Daisy as if they were his own kids, too. And his friendship with Savvy had not only been repaired, but had turned into something more. Or that was what he'd thought until last night when she'd told him to leave.

He should've told her about when he received Willow's letter. It would have been so much better if he'd have told her himself instead of her figuring it out on her own.

But Brodie had to make her realize that he truly had changed since he showed up at Willow's trailer that first day. He wanted to do the right thing by everyone, especially those he cared

about most, which included Dylan, Rose, Daisy…
and undeniably Savvy.

He'd awakened with a goal of seeing her first
thing this morning, arriving at the sporting-goods
store and asking her to hear him out. Then he'd
beg her to believe him when he said that he still
wanted to be a part of the kids' lives. And that he
wanted to be a part of her life, too.

But after the morning workouts, he'd received
a call from the athletic director asking they meet
over lunch to discuss staffing changes for the next
season. And the lunch had lasted two hours.

By the time he finally made it to the square, it
was a quarter before two. But he was here now
and even more determined to persuade Savvy
to accept his apology, acknowledge that he'd
changed and admit that their relationship had
blossomed to something well beyond friendship.
He didn't want to spend even a day away from
the kids…or from Savvy.

He entered Bowers Sporting Goods and found
Savvy's grandmother organizing a rack of life
jackets. Assuming Savvy was working in the
back, he asked, "Mrs. Bowers, can I talk to Savvy
for a few minutes?" He knew Savvy would leave
soon to get home for the kids, but he didn't want
to wait any longer to talk to her. He'd been waiting all day.

Jolaine Bowers frowned. "Oh, my, I'd assumed she was with you. You haven't seen her today, then?"

Brodie shook his head. "No, not at all. You thought she was with me?"

She placed the last jacket on the rack and nodded. "She called this morning asking if she could have the day off because she needed to talk to someone, and I thought that she probably meant you. Can't imagine who else she'd have needed to talk to." Her eyebrows puckered as she apparently checked off potential folks and came up empty.

Brodie didn't know who the person was either, but he wouldn't waste any more time here looking for Savvy. She'd be at the trailer soon, and he'd see her there. "I'll find her," he said. "Thanks anyway."

"Of course. We really loved seeing the two of you together Sunday," she added. "I think you're good for our Savvy."

Brodie smiled. "Thanks." He thought he was good for Savvy, too, and that she was very good for him. He just had to convince her of the fact.

He left the store and walked to his truck, but quick steps approaching behind him caused him to turn…and find an angry woman had followed him away from the square.

She didn't bother with hello. "So? Are you

going to step up now? After Wendy's gone? A little late, isn't it?"

"Mrs. Jackson?" Brodie asked.

Willow's mother glared at him. "She thought you were going to come in and save the day a few months ago. Told me that you were going to be in her life now. I think she actually believed it until the end. I told your girlfriend that yesterday." She shook her head. "The two of you weren't anything but trouble for Wendy."

She'd talked to Savvy yesterday? And told her…what, exactly? "Mrs. Jackson, I don't know what you're talking about," he said calmly, because she certainly wasn't calm.

"I'm talking about you, and the fact that you were never there for her, all of those years. She was on her own, and neither of you did anything but get her in trouble and then leave her be. You, especially, living your big fancy baseball dreams while Wendy barely scraped by because *she* was raising *your* son."

Brodie's shock couldn't have been stronger if she'd pulled out a gun and aimed it at his heart. "My *son*?"

Dylan's face overpowered Brodie's thoughts. The way they connected so easily. The things they had in common. The reminders of himself in the boy's actions, emotions, likes, dislikes. And the

memory of that night, when he'd left Willow...
and given up the chance to know his own son.

She tilted her face, sizing up his reaction, and
then she shook her head again. "Your girlfriend
didn't know," she said, her words slicing through
his heart. "But Wendy told you!"

"No," he whispered. "She didn't."

She jerked her head back, clearly not believing
him. "She did. She told me that you would be in
her life again soon."

Brodie thought of the letter, and the fact that
he hadn't answered it until it was too late. And
his heart clenched so hard that it hurt. What had
he done?

Lorina Jackson huffed out an exasperated
breath. "You knew," she said. "You had to have
known. Savvy didn't...I could tell she didn't. But
you." She wagged a finger at him. "Don't even
try to act like you didn't know. You were just too
into yourself to care about anyone else, especially
Wendy or your son. You never were any kind of
friend—or anything else—to my daughter. Not
you, or Savvy." Then she turned on her heel and
stomped away.

Leaving Brodie to sort out the information.
Dylan was his son. He knew it in his heart, even
though he'd never considered it before. Willow
had planned to tell him, but she'd died before
she could.

And the shocking fact that had been the final sucker punch to Brodie's world...

Savvy knew.

Savvy spent two hours at Brother Henry's office confirming what God had already put on her heart, that she needed to forgive Brodie and that she needed to tell him the truth about Dylan. Turn it over to God, as Brother Henry said, and stop assuming that because Brodie had made mistakes in the past, he'd continue to make the same mistakes in the future. She only needed to look in the mirror to realize the truth in that sentiment.

What if everyone in town had continued to judge her based on her own past?

Savvy needed to apologize profusely to Brodie. And then she also planned to tell him another prominent truth. Somewhere along the way over the past few weeks, she'd fallen completely in love with him.

She pulled up at the trailer at 3:15 p.m. to find him waiting, standing beside his truck. Her heart skittered at the sight of him, and she couldn't wait to tell him that she'd been wrong. Couldn't wait to apologize. Couldn't wait to tell him Dylan was his son. She tossed up a hand and smiled.

But he didn't return the gesture, and a shiver of fear trickled down her spine. She parked the truck and climbed out to face him, and then realized that she'd waited too long.

"You knew," he said, anger penetrating each word.

Savvy didn't have to ask what he meant. She could see it in the pain in his eyes, and the look of animosity directed solely at her. "I was going to tell you today," she said quickly. "I didn't know, not until yesterday, when I saw Lorina in the square. And then I…" She stumbled over what to say.

"You chose not to tell me," he said, his words sharp and clipped, "that Dylan was my son?"

"I was going to," she repeated, recalling everything she'd conveyed to Brother Henry over the past few hours, "but then I got so angry when I realized that you didn't answer Willow's letter and I was afraid that you'd hurt him or take him from me." Her words lodged in her throat as heat crept from his neck to his face.

"You were afraid I'd *hurt* him?" he asked incredulously. "My son? Why?" And then he closed his eyes. "You mean like I hurt Willow. And like I hurt you. Have mercy, Savvy, what would it take for you to believe that I've changed? And how dare you decide whether or not I deserve to know that Dylan is my son!" He scrubbed a weary hand across his face. "You saw how much I hated not being a part of Marissa's life. How could you even think about keeping me out of his?"

"I was wrong," she said. "I realized that today, and I've spent the whole afternoon with Brother Henry talking about it and seeing how terribly wrong I've been. I was going to tell you that I was sorry, so very sorry," she said, hot tears pushing free, "and I was going to tell you about Dylan."

Brodie's jaw flexed, those icy blue eyes cold and accusing, and Savvy didn't blame him.

"Where is Dylan?" he asked. "Why didn't the kids get off the bus?"

"The girls went home with Mandy after school," she said brokenly. "And Dylan has the baseball camp until five."

"Right," he said, turning toward his truck. "I'll be picking him up from the camp." He climbed into the truck without another word and left without looking back.

A loud blast of thunder caused her to jump as she made her way to the deck and collapsed on the steps. A storm was undoubtedly coming, and the heavy clouds beginning to claim the sky seemed appropriate for Savvy's world, suffocating the light completely as her tears fell and her chest heaved from the weight of her shattered heart.

Chapter Sixteen

Savvy couldn't remember a time she'd stayed outside purposefully as a storm came. But after Brodie had left and her world had fallen apart, she hadn't moved, feeling as though she somehow deserved the inner terror she experienced with every blast of thunder, every bolt of lightning.

The rain hadn't started yet, but it would come.

A loud crack signaled lightning had hit something in the distance, and Savvy nearly didn't hear her phone because of the sound. She pulled it from her pocket, saw Mandy's name on the display and answered, "Mandy? Are the girls okay?"

"They are, but when the storm started, they both started crying and said they needed to tell me their secret. Savvy, the girls said Dylan didn't go to school today."

"He— What?"

"They said he told them he wasn't going to

school. Apparently, he didn't get on the bus and went into the woods somewhere along the way to wait for the bus to leave. He didn't say where he was going, but he told them not to tell anyone, that it was a secret. And they didn't, until the storm started, and they became scared that he was out in it alone. I asked them if they knew why he missed school, and they said no."

Savvy could hear the girls crying in the background and saying they were sorry. She hated that she wasn't there to hold them and comfort them, but her first priority had to be Dylan. "So he's been gone all day?" she asked. He'd been upset after she told Brodie to leave and after learning Brodie had initially ignored Willow's letter. But obviously, she hadn't realized how much.

"Apparently so," Mandy sighed.

"He was upset with me," Savvy said, hurrying inside to retrieve her keys. She grabbed them from the counter and then started out. "And I didn't think anything about him not coming home today because he had the baseball camp." She realized Brodie would be arriving at the high school fields soon, if he wasn't already there, and would also realize Dylan was gone. "Mandy, I need to call Brodie and let him know."

"Good idea. He can help look for him, and I'll call Daniel and see if he and some of the other men from church can help, too. And, Savvy, we'll pray that we find him soon."

Savvy climbed into her truck. "Thanks," she said, praying as well as she disconnected and dialed Brodie.

"He isn't here," Brodie answered, his voice as gruff as it'd been when he left the trailer.

"I know," she said as another boom of thunder shook her truck. "Mandy just called. The girls told her that Dylan didn't get on the bus this morning, but they don't know where he went. Brodie, he heard us talking outside the trailer last night. He was mad at me for asking you to leave and—" She didn't want to tell him the rest.

"And at me?" he asked. "He heard I ignored Willow's letter, didn't he? And so he left?"

"Yes," Savvy admitted, her hand shaking as she held the phone to her ear. The storm was picking up speed, and Dylan was somewhere in it. "Brodie, I don't know what to do."

"I'll find him," he said, and Savvy suspected he was about to hang up. She didn't want to deal with this on her own, and she didn't know where to look for an upset teenager.

"Wait! Brodie, please, don't hang up. Let me help. Let me search for him with you." She waited as the rain started to fall. "Please, Brodie. I love him, and I don't have any idea where he could've gone, and the storm is coming. Brodie, I'm scared."

She heard the loud motor of his truck and knew that he'd already started driving to look for Dylan. The thought of the boy on his own, alone and maybe in trouble, or hurt—or who knew what?— had her heart racing, and she begged again. "Please, Brodie."

"Meet me at the Cutters' place," he said. "I think I know where he is." Then he hung up, and Savvy pressed her foot to the floor and steered her truck toward the Cutters' farm, realizing where they were going and knowing Brodie was probably right. The Cutter property wasn't that far from the trailer. She'd be there in minutes. But that property provided the easiest path to the place Willow, Brodie and Savvy had spent so much time together. And the place where Dylan had last been with his mom.

Jasper Falls.

Brodie's wipers beat heavily against his windshield as the rain increased, falling in thick sheets as he made his way to the Cutters' place. If Dylan had gone where he suspected, he could be in all kinds of trouble. Because unlike the last time that Brodie had found him in the storm, this time he'd have likely reached his destination. And Jasper Falls was no place for a teenager in a storm. Too many jagged protrusions, slick moss-covered flat rocks and the water itself, increasing in volume and intensity as the rain fell.

Brodie could very well lose his son before he ever got the chance to tell him he was his father. "God, please, keep him safe," he prayed. "I love him, You know I do. Don't let me lose him, Lord. Please."

I love him.

Savvy's words echoed his own, and he gripped the steering wheel tighter. If she'd told him the truth last night, this might not have happened.

No. No, he wouldn't blame Savvy for this. That'd be doing the same thing she'd done to him, when she'd blamed him for ignoring Willow's letter. He hadn't caused Willow's death. And Savvy hadn't caused Dylan to run away. Placing blame now wouldn't do anybody any good. The only thing that would...was prayer.

So he continued silently praying as he drove up the Cutters' driveway and saw Savvy climbing out of her truck in the rain. She was crying, her face panic-stricken as she glanced toward the trail that led to the falls and then back at Brodie. She wore the same thin T-shirt and jeans she'd had on earlier, and he knew she'd left immediately, not even taking time to grab a jacket, because she wanted to find Dylan as badly as Brodie did.

He had been so angry at her, not wanting to talk

to her or even look at her when he left the trailer. But now, seeing her worried—distraught—over Dylan…over his son… Brodie's anger subsided and he only felt one thing: determination to find the boy they both loved.

She hurried toward him as he got out of the truck. "Brodie, I'm so sorry. This is all my fault, and I hate myself for it. Please forgive me. I don't know what I'll do if anything happens to him." Her words came out in a rush, her eyes blinking through the combination of rain and tears.

"It isn't your fault, Savvy." He grabbed his jacket from the backseat and handed it to her. "And I do forgive you," he said, meaning every word.

She took the jacket, hurriedly slipped it on. "I mean it, Brodie. I'm so, so sorry."

He placed his hand on her chin, focused on those dark, sad eyes. "I believe you," he said huskily. "And I forgive you. And that's what you and I are going to start doing from now on, believing each other and forgiving each other, right?"

She blinked, nodded.

"But right now we're going to find my son," he said. "Come on." Then he led the way toward the trail.

Savvy gripped Brodie's hand fiercely as she slipped for the fifth time, her ankle twisting as her foot flipped over against the slippery rock. Like every other time, he helped her right herself and then continued, and she followed at the same swift pace, knowing that every minute could make a difference in how they found Dylan. How long had he been here, and where at Jasper Falls would he be? There were so many dangerous areas surrounding the falls. And there was always the possibility that he had slipped, and…

No, dear God. Please, don't let him die the way Willow did. Let him be okay.

"Almost there," Brodie said, moving even faster as Savvy tried to keep up, the sound of the rushing water overpowering the thunder.

Savvy's prayers hadn't stopped—her thanking God for Brodie allowing her to help him look for Dylan, and for Brodie's forgiveness, and for giving her the chance to raise Willow's children. She thanked and prayed and begged continually, the conversation with God ongoing, until they rounded that final curve, and Brodie stopped in his tracks.

"Dylan!" he yelled, and Savvy looked up to see what Brodie saw, Dylan, his back pushed against the highest precipice with the forceful water gushing merely inches away. That had been the very spot he and Willow were trying to reach when she fell, and Brodie knew, as Savvy did, how slick that rock became when the waterfall increased. How

Dylan kept from sliding off was beyond Savvy. "Stay right there!" Brodie yelled. "I'm coming!"

Dylan nodded, and Savvy prayed, "Oh, God, please, keep him safe." Then she said to Brodie, "He must have wanted to get to that spot where she'd planned to tell him who his father was."

Brodie's jaw flexed again, but she knew it wasn't out of anger this time, and he nodded. "Help us, Lord," he prayed, then turned to Savvy. "I'm going up to get him. If anything happens, you go for help. Understand?"

"Yes." She'd never been able to climb to the top, even without rain. Then Brodie released her hand, and a fear like nothing she'd ever experienced rushed through her. What if she lost both of them? "Brodie," she called out, causing him to turn. "Don't you die up there. I—I love you."

The hint of a smile lifted his mouth. "I don't plan to," he said, "but keep praying. And I love you, too."

Brodie was thankful he wore hiking boots instead of tennis shoes, because even with the boots, he had a difficult time finding traction on the severe rocks leading to the top of the falls. He didn't want to think of how Dylan had navigated his way to the top without anyone around to help him if he fell.

Then again, Brodie remembered doing the

same thing a time or two when he'd been about that age. His son indeed. His foot slipped on a moss-covered overhang, and Brodie lost his balance, falling into a tree growing from the edge of the falls and grunting as a sharp branch jabbed into his back.

"Coach, you okay?" Dylan yelled.

"Yeah," Brodie returned, and saw that the kid had leaned forward to see what had happened. "Keep your back against the rock until I'm there."

"Yes, sir," Dylan answered, his face disappearing as he followed Brodie's command.

His son. Brodie shot a glance down to see Savvy, her hands shielding her eyes from the rain as she watched his progress. She saw him and held up the okay sign, her way of asking if everything was all right.

Brodie looked up, realized he was merely feet from Dylan, and nodded. Everything was very okay. God was with them. Brodie could feel Him right beside him through every difficult step in the climb. And after another step of faith across a water-covered ledge, he cleared the top and saw his son.

"Dylan," he said, moving toward the drenched teenager. "Are you okay? Is anything hurt?"

"No," Dylan said, frowning, "but I made it up here before the rain, and then, once the falls got heavier and the rain got harder, I…"

Brodie had never been able to admit when he was scared, either. "I get it," he said.

"I was mad at you, and at Aunt Savvy," Dylan admitted. "So I skipped school and came up here. I'm sorry." He looked away from Brodie as though he thought Brodie would begin a reprimand for his actions. Maybe someday that was what Brodie would do as this boy's father. But today wasn't that day. Today he would follow through with what Dylan wanted the first time he'd planned to come to this very spot.

"This was where your mom was going to tell you about your dad," Brodie said, moving closer, and then sitting beside Dylan on the ledge, thankful that the rain had begun to slack off.

Dylan squinted up at Brodie. He was probably wondering why Brodie didn't start figuring out how the two of them were going to climb down, but Brodie wasn't worried about that now. God helped him get here; He'd help him bring Dylan down. But God was giving him an opportunity to give Dylan what he wanted, and give Brodie what he wanted at the same time. "She never got to tell me," Dylan finally said.

"Dylan, I want to tell you first that I didn't know who your father was when I came here. I had no idea." He watched as Dylan leaned forward, eager to hear anything Brodie had to say about his dad.

"But do you know now, Coach?" he asked. "Did you find out who my dad is?"

"I did," Brodie said. "Just a couple of hours ago, and I tried to find you so I could tell you then." He couldn't stop the smile that eased out freely as he took in the magnitude of this moment, sitting beside his son and telling him that he was his father. "I'm…" he started, but he didn't say the words before Dylan's eyes widened.

"Coach?" he asked. "Are—are you my dad?"

"I didn't know, Dylan, or I'd never have left you and your mom alone all those years. But your mom's letter asking me to come help you, I know now that she'd planned to do more than that. She'd planned to tell me the truth so that I could have a place in your life, so that I could be the dad I want to be for you," he said, his voice cracking with emotion. "I understand if you're angry that I wasn't around—" And again, before he could continue, Dylan broke in, his smile bursting free in spite of the rain still dripping down his face.

"I'm not angry," Dylan said. "I'm— I've got a dad." His grin managed to somehow grow wider. "And he's a college baseball coach," he added, the hint of laughter playing through the words. "How cool is that?"

Brodie laughed as well, and he scooted closer to him, wrapped an arm around him and enjoyed the feel of the boy who already felt like such an intense part of him.

And then Brodie caught movement at the bottom of the falls. Savvy had undoubtedly seen the interaction, and she jumped wildly, waving her arms. "Everything okay?" she yelled, but her smile said she knew that it was.

Brodie and Dylan waved back, and Dylan replied before Brodie had a chance.

"Everything's great!" he said as several men led by Daniel Brantley, Landon and John Cutter emerged from the pathway behind Savvy.

She said something to the group and then yelled, "They're going to help y'all get down!"

"Awesome!" Brodie yelled back, and then he turned toward his son, who was still grinning. "But it's pretty nice up here, isn't it?"

Dylan nodded. "Pretty awesome," he said, and then smiled as he added, "Dad."

Two hours later, the rescue team had left, Dylan was taking a hot shower in Landon Cutter's log cabin and Brodie and Savvy sat in two rocking chairs on the front porch while they waited on Dylan to finish.

Savvy had so much she wanted to say, but she started with what seemed the most important. "So you really forgive me for not telling you yesterday?"

"I told you I forgive you," he said, "and I meant it. That's something we're going to make sure we do for each other from now on, in this relationship."

"This relationship," she repeated, loving the sound of the words on his lips. And also remembering what he'd told her before he started the climb to get to Dylan.

He reached over and pulled her hand, urging her out of her rocker and into his lap. Then he grinned and kissed her, softly at first and then more significantly, until Savvy forgot where they were and only thought about how very much she loved this man.

"I love you, Savvy Bowers," he said, once the kiss ended.

"I love you, too," she murmured, and then laughed as he kissed her again, first on the lips and then the forehead, and then smothered kisses all over her face and neck. "And I'm not mad. I'm ecstatic. This is perfect. Our family…is going to be perfect."

"Our family," she repeated, tears falling, but these were tears of absolute joy.

"You, me, Dylan and the girls. I came to the square today to find you and convince you to forgive me and to understand that this is what I want more than anything. I'd planned to tell you that I'll try not to let you down again," he said.

"And that I'll do my best to be a good husband, and a good father, if you'll let me be a part of your lives. Yours, and Dylan's, and Rose's and Daisy's. I love you all."

"Husband?" she whispered.

He continued the sporadic kisses while she giggled. "Marry me, Savvy. And then we can go tell the kids."

Laughing, she asked, "Tell them what, exactly?"

"That we're going to be a family. A real family. The kind you talked about when we were teens, the kind you said you always wanted. And the kind I never even realized that I want more than anything. Until you." He winked, kissed her again. "How does that sound, Sav?"

"It sounds," she said, truly amazed at the blessings God had given, "perfect."

Epilogue

Six months later

"Hey, Dad, will you fix my tie?"

Brodie looked at Dylan's attempt at knotting the blue silk tie and grinned. "I never could tie one of these when I was your age, either."

Dylan smiled. "Guess we've got that in common, too, huh?"

Brodie nodded. "I guess so." He fixed the tie, and then lifted an eyebrow. "I thought we said you were going to visit Mr. Crowe before the wedding."

Dylan slung the long hair out of his face and smirked. "I did visit him. I just didn't get a haircut."

"So I need to start choosing my words better when I ask you to do something, is that what you're saying?" Brodie asked wryly.

"Pretty much," Dylan said, then shrugged. "Ella Kate likes it," he added, referencing his current crush, a girl he'd started talking to the first day of high school. He'd been almost as excited about starting high school as the girls had been about moving up to first grade.

"So, if Ella Kate likes the long hair, it stays, even though I recommended a cut?" Brodie asked.

"And Marissa said she thought it was cool, too. You aren't going to argue with her, are you?"

"I'm not arguing with anybody," Brodie answered, "especially not my daughter." It thrilled him to know that Ryan and Cherie sat in the pews of the church, and that Savvy had asked Marissa to be her maid of honor. The teenager had said she was honored, but Brodie was moved beyond words.

The music changed, and laughter echoed from the auditorium.

"Rose and Daisy are walking in," Dylan said, easing the door open so that he and Brodie could see the twins.

Brodie also laughed at the pair. Wearing matching blue dresses, they were skipping down the aisle as if they were on their way to a party. And Brodie knew...they were.

A big party, orchestrated by God, that would include all of their friends and family...and the woman he loved, who, he realized, would be walking down the aisle soon.

"Hey, I think we're supposed to go out now," Dylan said. "Marissa is already halfway down the aisle."

"Right behind you, son," Brodie said, still enjoying calling him that. And after today, he'd also have two precious daughters.

Thank You, God.

Brodie and Dylan took their places beside Brother Henry and watched as Savvy, wearing her grandmother's lace wedding gown, started down the aisle. She captured his gaze and held it while Brodie admired the woman who would be his for life, and the beauty of the blessings God had bestowed.

Brodie knew he wasn't supposed to speak yet, but when she reached the front of the church, he couldn't hold back. "You are an amazing bride."

And apparently, Dylan couldn't hold back, either. "Aunt Savvy?"

Savvy looked toward him. "Yes, Dylan?"

"You're a pretty cool mom, too."

Her hand moved to her throat, and her lip trembled. "Thank you, Dylan."

"Aunt Savvy?" Rose asked, apparently deciding that it was okay to talk now, even though this wasn't how the rehearsal had been.

"Yes, Rose?" Savvy murmured.

"Are you our new mommy now?"

"Can we call you Mommy after y'all kiss?" Daisy chimed in.

Savvy swallowed. "If that's what you want."

They both nodded and smiled. Then Dylan added, "It's what we all want."

Brodie wasn't sure what to say, his heart filling with love for his new family. And Savvy seemed speechless, too.

So Brother Henry cleared his throat and asked, "Brodie? Savvy?" He looked at Dylan, Rose and Daisy and then added, "Daddy and Mommy..." He paused. "Are we ready to begin?"

Brodie took Savvy's hand, and then he held his other out to Dylan, who grabbed on. Then Savvy motioned for the girls, who scooted close and held on to Savvy's bouquet-laden arm.

Brother Henry smiled.

"We're ready to begin," Brodie said, and his bride, looking at him with more love than he'd ever thought he deserved, added, "Beyond ready."

* * * * *

Dear Reader,

In the spring of 2013, Alanus and Jerry, ages four and five, lost their mommy and daddy within three months of each other, their father to cancer, their mother to a heart attack. Their parents were young, and their passing didn't make sense. But, as Dylan, Rose and Daisy learned, sometimes God needs people in heaven.

Our son and daughter-in-law had only been married eight months when God put on their hearts to adopt our precious grandboys. I can't express how our family loves those boys, or how our community and our church embraced them and loved them through something no child should ever experience.

Because of their story, I wanted to write Dylan, Rose and Daisy's story, to show a community pulling together for orphaned children. It's a beautiful, touching thing to experience, and I found myself crying through several of the scenes, not only for the children, but for Savvy, who had so far to go in learning that forgiveness has no limits. She and Brodie touched my heart, and I hoped they touched yours, as well.

My next book will begin a series about the child home Brodie and Savvy start in Willow's honor. More information and discussion questions for book clubs are available on my website, www.reneeandrews.com, Facebook page, www.facebook.com/AuthorReneeAndrews, and Twitter, @ReneeAndrews. And you'll see pictures of Alanus and Jerry there, too. See if their smiles don't put one on your face, too. I know they keep a smile on mine! If you have prayer requests, let me know. I'll lift your request up to the Lord in prayer. I love to hear from readers, so please write to me at renee@reneeandrews.com or at P.O. Box 8, Gadsden, AL 35902.

Blessings in Christ,
Renee Andrews

LARGER-PRINT BOOKS!

GET 2 FREE LARGER-PRINT NOVELS PLUS 2 FREE MYSTERY GIFTS

Love Inspired®
SUSPENSE
RIVETING INSPIRATIONAL ROMANCE

Larger-print novels are now available...

Reader Service.com

Manage your account online!
- Review your order history
- Manage your payments
- Update your address

> *We've designed
> the Harlequin® Reader Service
> website just for you.*

Enjoy all the features!
- Reader excerpts from any series
- Respond to mailings and special monthly offers
- Discover new series available to you
- Browse the Bonus Bucks catalog
- Share your feedback

Visit us at:
ReaderService.com

RS13